D0436466

The
House
of Silence

The

House

of Silence

BLANCA BUSQUETS

Translation by Mara Faye Lethem

Regan Arts.

NEW YORK

Regan Arts.

65 Bleecker Street
New York, NY 10012

First Regan Arts hardcover edition, October 2016

Library of Congress Control Number: 2016939705

ISBN 978-1-68245-030-7

Interior design by Nancy Singer
Cover design by Chin-Yee Lai

Printed in the United States of America

10 9 8 7 6 5 4 3 2 1

To my father and my Uncle Francesc,
for whom music means everything.

The
Rehearsal

Teresa

I found the first violin in a garbage dump. And it was an excellent violin, even though I obviously didn't know that yet. What I did know was that it was a magical violin. I saw that right away, just by looking at it, because it was shining in the dusk, and things that shine are usually magic. I'm not making that up. Mother and I would often rummage through the dump to see if we could find something that we could sell. If I told that to some of the people here with me now, they would be shocked.

In fact, until now I was alone here, in the theater I mean. And then, all of a sudden, I heard some soft footsteps approaching the stage entrance, announcing the appearance of the first musician. He's a drab trumpeter, with a face that suggests the only thing in the world he has of any value is his trumpet. He greets me with a wave and says something I don't catch. I think he's Romanian; I vaguely remember someone telling me that.

I had been looking out at the empty seats for some time, sitting with the violin in my hand, because I was tired of warming up and missed the silence. The silence of the empty theater and the silence outside in this city, in the squares, on the streets. A silence of dead leaves. From the hotel window, before coming here, I saw leaves fall, leaves that carpet the colorful ground in autumn. Where I live—Catalonia—I'd have to go to the mountains to see colors like these. Mountains I didn't visit until I was a teenager, because as a girl I could never afford to leave Barcelona.

Everything changed after I found the violin. Look what I found, I said, triumphantly lifting the instrument in one hand and the bow in the other. And as I lifted it, I brushed my hand over the strings without meaning to, and they made a rending, high-pitched sound that wrenched at my soul. It was a strange sound and I wasn't sure I whether I liked it. Then I took a good look at the violin and I stared into one F-hole, which of course I didn't know was called that, because all I saw was a long opening—at the bottom of it there were some handwritten letters. I was able to read them, but I couldn't understand them. I made out a date: 1672. What are you looking at? complained my mother. Let's take it; that we can sell. Mother never paid attention to the shape of things we pulled from the dump; she only focused on what they were made of, to see if someone would pay any money for them. It wasn't that we lived on the street or in absolute poverty, or maybe we did; it depends on how you look at it. Yes, definitely, if you look at it with today's eyes—because now everyone's expected to have a balanced diet, with fruit, vegetables, carbohydrates, and I don't even know what else. Then, our balanced diet was whatever we had, and one day there might have only been bread and a bit of cheese, or some chickpeas or lentils. My father (according to my mother—I never met him) was a foreigner who came to Barcelona, made love to her a few nights in a row, and then left again. And mother, who could more or less get by, found herself with a baby to feed. And back then getting by wasn't so simple.

That's why you're blonde and have blue eyes. Like him, she would say, stroking my cheek softly with the back of her fingers. She told me that from a very young age, and I saw how, sometimes, she would look at me and cry, perhaps because she still felt bound to that man who came with the north wind and left with the south, after depositing a magical seed that would grow and end up being me. When Mother told me that I was like him, that I had his eyes and his hair, I didn't know whether I should love him or miss him, or whether I should hate him for what he'd done. It was a tentative feeling, nothing seemed clear, I had no idea what was true and what was a lie. I had the same feeling when I found Karl many years later.

I remember that day at the dump, when we'd gone later than usual, because I remember that it got dark on us, and I thought, *What's this? It looks like a wooden box.* It was hidden among the garbage and hard to see. And then I rescued it from underneath all that, and when I realized it was a violin, I instinctively, eagerly, searched for the bow beside it. It wasn't that I had seen many violins in my life, but I'd seen one in a book my teacher had read to us at school. In it a girl played the violin with her eyes closed, and, without having ever heard the sound, I could imagine it playing inside my head, and the strangest thing is that it really sounded like a violin. By that I mean that when I actually heard one for the first time, I realized that it was the same sound I had imagined. And the first time I played it, I closed my eyes, like the girl in the book. Later, I would open them ridiculously wide as I struggled to follow along with those Baroque composers who put even the most virtuoso players to the test, trying to draw out those dizzying melodies that were like a roller coaster.

But that would be much later. That day, at seven years old, having a violin of my own changed my life. Bring it over, come on, it's really late, my mother had insisted. And I had to put the violin in the little cart we used to transport what we gathered each afternoon. She would put down her sewing and pick me up at school, and then we'd go for a stroll through the dump. Afterwards, we would bring what we found to the rag-and-bone man, and he kept what he thought he could resell. He gave us a coin or two, and that coin would ensure that we'd be able to eat the next day. Sometimes mother got paid on delivery for the clothes she sewed, and other times, she only saw the money after much insisting. I never went hungry, because she somehow always managed to give me something to eat. But she had gone hungry before she thought up selling stuff to the rag-and-bone man.

Barcelona in those days was the flip side of today's Berlin, with its colorful leaves. Barcelona was a dark city, still too close to a war that had stripped its inhabitants of their will to live, and still too far from the student uprisings that would change the city's atmosphere. There wasn't even television yet.

I had a magic violin, though. We reached the ragman's shop, and I planted myself in front of the cart before we went in. Please, please, don't sell the violin, I said, bringing my hands together to plead my case. Mother looked at me with surprise: But Teresa, we could make a pretty penny with this. Yes, I've always wanted to be a violinist, I made up on the spot. Mother softened her expression: Oh, really, I didn't know. You never told me that. Please, I insisted.

We took the violin home. I had never thought about being a violinist, obviously—but at school there was the book about the girl who played the violin with her eyes closed, and I had found this instrument that seemed magical. I felt music taking shape within me, music which would be a part of me from then on. It came up from deep inside, as if filling my mouth with melodies—and then I thought, *Yes, I had to be a violinist.*

Maria

"Maria, don't fall back to sleep!"

"No, I'm not sleeping, I'm coming . . ."

Now they want me to rush because they want to start the rehearsal, and I'm lagging behind. My stomach's been hurting for days, and I'm too old to rush around. I'm old, Mr. Karl, I'm old.

Now I'll have to hear that music again, that music I've heard so many times I know it by heart; music that tears me up inside and makes me want to cry—and I haven't cried in some time. But they promised me I'll hear it from a red theater seat, like a real lady—and it turns out that I, who never wanted to be a lady, will be one whether I like it or not. It was Mr. Mark who promised me this, obviously, since Mrs. Anna won't even look at me and wants nothing to do with me.

Yesterday I took a plane. I'd never done that before, and it was terrible. I didn't like not having my feet on the floor, not at all. You don't know where you are; you don't know what's going on. And I still have to take another one to get home. It's times like this when all I can do is leave it in the hands of Our Lady of Hope, the Blessed Holy Virgin of the Macarena!

I don't know this city and I find it strange, but on the other hand it seems that everything here gives off the scent of Mr. Karl—a smell that bewilders me, that makes me keenly aware of everything happening around me. I told Mr. Mark that I don't want to leave the hotel alone, because I'm sure I'll get lost. Then stay here, Maria, he had replied, or go back to your sister's; weren't you with her yesterday? Oh, yes, but she has to work, I said, stalling, I'll stay here; I'll stay here until it's time for the rehearsal. And that is what I did. But tomorrow I'll have to go out again and I'll have to dress up for the concert, like some opera singer, like the one who used to come by the house. And tomorrow I'll have to do what I planned.

When Mr. Karl asked me if I wanted to learn to play the violin or the piano, I was shocked. What are you saying, sir? And I remembered the priest in my town in Andalusia, who made you sing at your First Communion whether you wanted to or not. Otherwise, he wouldn't let you take communion. A little bit, just a little, he would say. And then you'd sing, that song that goes *Qué alegría cuando me dijeron: vamos a la casa del Señor* . . . Well, now that nobody's around to hear, I can admit that I was really quite good at it. And then I really got into it, and I started singing in the shower, and then on the street. Later, when I came to Barcelona, I always sang as I cleaned the houses of those two gussied-up ladies, the homes I worked in before Mr. Karl's. And then, when I ended up at his house, and it turned out that he could pay me well and it was a good house, I started to sing there too. And he played the piano at the other end of the house, constantly. So, I sang louder, more and more, because I couldn't hear myself singing those love songs that touched my soul and made me feel so good. There was one that went *Linda paloma miiiia, ven hacia miiii*... And that was the one I liked best and sang most often, and I would even cry with emotion when I did. And I sang it louder and louder until finally I could no longer hear the piano because I'd managed to lose myself in the song. Well, that was what I thought, but really it was that Mr. Karl had stopped playing. On that very first day he stuck his head through the door and put a finger to his lips and said shhhh. And it really stung, since I thought that he was coming over to compliment me on my voice. I closed my mouth at once, and I didn't open it again while Mr. Karl was around the house, because I didn't want to lose my job, but also because I was offended. And he was always there, with the violin or with the piano, always one thing or the other. I always sang when he was out, until one day he caught me singing and asked whether I wanted to learn to play the piano or the violin, I could choose. I felt my cheeks turn bright red and so hot that I couldn't stand it. When I tensely said, no thank you, he seemed disappointed.

Mr. Karl was the kind of man who turned heads. I found him immediately attractive when we met, and he told me that he'd just moved to Barcelona and needed a maid. He said if I wanted a job, I should go see him. I went and he opened the door and he said hello, and that was all, because he didn't know how to say anything more in any language I could understand. But I've always been very clever, and I quickly understood what he wanted when he explained it in gestures. Then he showed me a room with a bed and a bathroom, right near the kitchen. Ay, Holy Weeping Virgin! I had never worked in a house like that one, and I had never spent the night. And that man wanted me to live there. I started to have doubts, but they only lasted a few minutes, until he put some numbers in front of my nose on a piece of paper, astronomical numbers I'd never seen before either, plus one full day off each week. That was more than I could ever have anywhere else. Agreed, I said without any further discussion. In my head, I was already thinking about what I could do with all that money. I could buy all the chocolate I wanted, and clothes, I could even buy myself some jewelry, a good ring or maybe even some earrings—and, what's more, I wouldn't have expenses because I'd be living in someone else's house. Mr. Karl held out a hand for me to shake and I was surprised, but I placed mine in his. That was new for me, too. He was so strong. I almost screamed from the pain of his grip. But I didn't scream, no. I tolerated it and I stayed.

That was the house of silence. Music played, but it played at a distance, Mr. Karl would close himself up in a room and do his thing, I mean he played the violin or the piano, or both, or he'd sing too, and he sang very loudly. One day I saw that afterwards he would write down notes on a piece of paper. I didn't understand what that was, but I didn't dare ask. He looked into my eyes and said, I'm composing, Maria. But that was when we started speaking to each other. Because at first we didn't speak at all, no. At first it seemed that Mr. Karl didn't want to tell me anything about what I should or shouldn't do. I would ask him, sir, what can I do for you? And he wouldn't hear me or pretended not to. Finally he said, I hired you to do what you think needs to be done; I don't have time to think. Okay, sir, I said, and I left and I thought, *Maria, make a list of what needs to be done in this house, because from now on it's as if it were yours.* The same thing happened when I went to get my wages for the first time. I saw how the days passed and Mr. Karl didn't pay me, and, when I had been there for two months and hadn't seen a dime, I got the nerve up to say something. And he had me follow him to a desk, and he took a small key out of a jar and opened up a drawer. And I saw that there was money there, a lot of money. I didn't say a word, but my eyes were like saucers. Here, he said, take your pay every month; I never remember these things. And, if some month there isn't enough, let me know. Okay, sir, I said again. Then he left and there I was alone, grabbing my month's pay myself, and thinking, *I could take it all right now and never come back.* But after considering the temptation briefly, I decided that I was no thief, and I forgot about it. I closed the drawer, turned the key, and put it back in the jar. I looked at my money and realized I still didn't have enough to buy any jewelry, but I could buy some chocolate just for me.

Teresa

After the trumpet player, they all start to show up. Everyone except Anna and Mark. They are late. Instinctively, I imitate the violinists in the orchestra, putting my violin on my shoulder to tune it. Now there is no longer silence. Later, if I have time, I'll go over the difficult passages, when the violin plays that wonderful game of tag with Bach's notes. And I already know that, once I get started, the concert will bring tears to my eyes and fill my heart with sadness. It will remind me of the last time we played it, here, and also of the day Karl invited me to his house to play with him for the first time. He told me, I've heard you play, and you perform Bach the way I believe he should be played.

Karl has been dead for ten years, but sometimes it doesn't seem that long ago; it seems that he'll come back today, to tell me not to put so much of my soul into it. Well, if you don't want me to put my soul into it, why did you ask me to play? I said one day, in exasperation. He looked into my eyes and replied, because it's easier to take out a bit of soul than to try to add it in. And there are very few people who put soul into their music.

If there was one thing I've always put in, it's soul. Music made me cry. Of course, today, I'll have trouble staying calm, but for many years the moment I started to play I was wiping away tears. I cried at seven years old, the day I brought the violin home with my mother's permission, even though I didn't even know how to properly hold the instrument, nor how it should sound. I looked again at the letters inside it, and I still didn't understand them. I only understood the 1672, and I tried to remember the drawing of the girl who played the violin in the book. I tried to remember how she held it, and I lifted it to my shoulder before running the bow over the strings. The result was an electrifying sound, slightly flat but deep, a sound that enthralled me and left me breathless. I never understood how someone, in times of hardship, could throw away such a valuable violin. It had even been more or less in tune, and the bow's strings were taut when I found that.

Mother and I lived in an apartment that was just a bathroom, a kitchen, and a bedroom. All our belongings were there, piled up in a corner because there was no closet. But none of our things were as valuable as the sewing machine, which was our means of survival and the only thing Mother hadn't sold when she'd had to leave the apartment where she'd lived with my grandparents until she was left all alone. A few years later, I was born. With the money she made from her sewing, she'd been able to rent that little place where I was born and grew up, and where I always had a bit of bread in the mornings and a small plate of food on the table at lunch and dinner. It wasn't much, but every once in a while, the neighbors would give me a piece of compound chocolate, which at the time I thought was delicious. If I ate it now, I'd probably retch. Sometimes, Mother was too busy working to eat, and she sewed and sewed while I ate my lunch or my dinner. If there was nothing left to sew, she cleaned. I watched her nervously work, with my mouth full, even though I quickly finished off my plate—which never really had that much on it to begin with. I would watch her until, one day, she fell to the floor before my very eyes. I screamed—I must have been five years old, and Mother was my whole world. I shook her a little bit: Mother, Mother. And she didn't react. I had heard her hit her head as she fell, and I was so scared that I went running to look for the neighbors, the ones who sometimes gave me compound chocolate. I knocked frantically on their door, and I started to cry. When they opened up, I could only say, Mother is on the floor, I don't know what's wrong with her—in fits and starts, sobbing and hiccupping, terrified: Mother is on the floor with her eyes closed. I couldn't get my brain around it; mothers aren't supposed to fall to the floor. They had come in, both the man and the woman, and he had run to call a doctor while she tried to get my mother to respond. When the doctor arrived she'd been murmuring for a bit and asking what had happened to her. Then, they sent me out, but as they pushed me toward the next-door neighbor's house, where there was a woman and her son whom I sometimes played with, I heard the doctor saying, this, ma'am, has but one name—and that's hunger.

The neighbors fed us for a few days. They didn't have extra money, but the man worked—and, at least, they had enough to eat. Mother was so weak that she couldn't sew while she was recovering. Now what will you do? the neighbor lady asked her in a whisper when she thought I couldn't hear. At first mother began to cry—but then she said: As soon as I get better, I'll find something;

the girl needs me strong. And that was how Mother thought up our work at the dump.

Bach consumes me. Mark always looks me straight in the eye to tell me to start the first note, my job; the first note has always been my job since Mother died. She didn't die then; she couldn't afford to yet; she still had to raise me. She died a few years later, when I was already teaching at the conservatory and was no longer cleaning apartments—because for a while I cleaned like she did. By then our trips to the dump had stopped. There were ladies who looked for women to clean their apartments at the other end of the city, and they wanted you to work by the hour, a few each day. You would arrive there and do everything: iron, wash dishes, clean bathrooms. Then you'd pick up the kids after school and take them to the park for a little while.

I cleaned apartments and I played the violin.

Maria

Mrs. Anna made sure to put down her violin case so that it rammed into my legs. I guess she does that to make me complain, but I'll never complain about not fitting into a taxi because of a violin, even if it's the Stainer. She does everything in her power to make my life impossible. I suppose she does it so I'll leave. She doesn't know that I can't leave now; I have to stay, because I have a job to do.

I made a mistake and threw the good violin into the trash. I don't know how it happened. I mean, I know how it happened—because, really, he was the one who made the mistake: Throw out the violin that's on the chair, he told me. I grabbed the violin that was on the chair and I threw it out. Now that I'm so slow to do anything, now that I drag behind as we walk to the taxi that will take us to the theater with the strange name—like everything in this city—I think of how quickly I grabbed that violin, and I went and threw it into the cart with all the trash. I was singing, since I was out of the house and he couldn't hear me. And I went back to the house singing, calm as could be. Now when I think of it, my hair stands on end. Especially when I think about what Mr. Karl said.

He noticed a few hours later, when it was already time to go to sleep. Where is my Stainer, he said, because that was a violin that had a name and its name was Stainer, which was quite a mouthful. At the time I thought it was a very pretty name, but surprising for a violin. After a moment of shocked silence, I answered: Sir, you told me to throw it out. Then he was the one who was shocked. After looking at me incredulously, he let out: What are you saying, Maria? I told you to throw out the broken violin. He had a note of desperation in his voice, but I had no intention of letting myself be intimidated: No, sir, you told me to throw out the one on the chair, and that's the one I threw out. Then Mr. Karl began to say *O, mein Gott, O, mein Gott,* and he kept saying *mein Gott*, looking all over for the other violin until he found it beneath the piano. He lifted it up with both hands and said, this is the violin to be thrown out. Petrified, I looked at the violin that wasn't even a violin anymore because it was like inside out. Mr. Karl held it up in front of my face and told me: This is worthless; I left it out in the sun, and look. And I looked at it and it looked strange, like deformed, as if someone had sucked the lids from the inside. The truth is, if I hadn't been feeling such terror and regret, I would have burst into laughter at that ludicrous situation and that funny-looking violin.

Where is it? he said suddenly, meaning the good violin. He placed the destroyed instrument back where he had found it. In the trash, in the cart, I already told you, I said without blinking. Yes, but where does the cart go? he asked me. To the dump, I said, stupefied, and nothing more came out of my mouth. We both went out to the street and, when he looked at me questioningly, I told him in a thin voice, the dump is very far away. He stopped for a moment and I had my head lowered, but I could feel his eyes on the back of my neck. Then I saw that he was hailing a taxi, and I went into the taxi dressed as a maid, with apron, cap, and everything, because he pushed me inside it. He got in himself and ordered: to the dump. The taxi driver, without saying a word, took us there. It was far, out in the middle of nowhere, and the trip was horrible, because neither of us spoke. But Mr. Karl's leg moved on its own every once in a while, and it made me jump every time. We arrived, and Mr. Karl told the taxi driver to wait while we got out and looked over that immense pile of rubbish and stink. They must have already emptied all the carts in the city because there wasn't a single one there. It was very late. Come on, said Mr. Karl, and he took me to the very edge of the garbage. You couldn't see much. I knew there were people who rummaged through the trash, but they did it during the day. Now you couldn't see anything. But Mr. Karl didn't let that stop him: Go on, get in there, he told me. Who? Me? I asked in alarm. Yes. Mr. Karl didn't want to hear any excuses, I could see that. I picked up my skirt and took a step. And then another and then another. And that was how I went straight into that disgusting dump, something I had certainly never done before, not here and not in Andalusia and never again since. Virgin of the Macarena, help me, I whispered. And I started to pick through all kinds of rubbish with my hands, and I got all dirty, and everything smelled really rotten, but I had to find that violin. I rummaged through everything I could for a good long while—up and down, there where the carts were emptied out, and it turned out that the violin wasn't there. I felt lost, it's not here, sir, I finally said, rising out of the filth. I saw him backlit, dark. I couldn't make out the expression on his face. I only heard him say, Come back. I went back and I couldn't find him. Mr. Karl had gotten back to the taxi and I thought he'd forgotten about me. I didn't say anything, I let him leave and I thought I'd have to walk home, and I tripped and I fell facedown and split open my forehead. Then I saw that the taxi was still there and that the rear door was open, waiting for me. I leapt toward the car. Mr. Karl didn't even look at me. He was glued to the other window, with his hand furtively covering his nose the whole time, but his leg no longer moved of its own accord. The taxi driver gave me a look through the rear-view mirror—a look that made me think, *Maria, you must stink to high heaven.*

Reaching the house after a trip in silence, I went to my room and washed up, cleaning the wound on my forehead as best I could. Then I packed my suitcase. What a way to lose a good job, I said to myself sadly. I'd only been working there for six months, but I'd realized that I had found one of the best houses to serve. I was happy there, and it seemed that Mr. Karl had been pleased with me. But all good things come to an end. With my coat on and my suitcase in one hand, I went to say goodbye to Mr. Karl. I found him sitting on the sofa, looking up, sighing over the lost violin. I said: Sir, I'm terribly sorry about what happened; forgive me. He looked at me in surprise and asked: Where could you possibly be going at this hour? I'm leaving, I said, confused; I figured after what happened . . . He got up and addressed the piano saying, don't start with that nonsense now; I was the one who told you to throw out the violin on the chair. And take care of your forehead; you've got a gash.

Teresa

The harpsichordist needs help to move her instrument over a bit. Two cellists have gotten up to assist her, along with some other boy who came out of nowhere and looks like a Goliath. We always think that people who seem strong are—until, in the end, they prove themselves to be people. I thought my mother was strong until she showed me her weaknesses, that she needed to eat in order to live, like everyone else—and, what's more, that she needed someone to give her support. Someone who wasn't a little girl who was really a burden, who made her have to work more just to get by.

I learned to recognize strength in people's eyes. When I met Karl, I saw strength in his. That wasn't my thought when I saw Anna's eyes, despite her showing up for the first time all sassy and ready to take on the world. She came with a maid, who took her around everywhere. Normally, at least for the first class, the parents would come to introduce me to the child and tell me what their expectations were or simply to meet me. That never happened with Anna; she came with the maid on the first day, and every other day as well, and Anna was already old enough to get around on her own. The maid would wait for her outside, and I sometimes would stick my head out the window and watch as they walked toward the Diagonal to catch the bus—because, as the girl had explained to me, they lived on the other side of the city, near the park with the lake.

I had spent a lot of time at the park myself. I brought children there to play after cleaning their kitchen, after ironing and scrubbing their floors and bathrooms. I say bathrooms because those folks had two and, sometimes, three—for me, that was quite the luxury. I had never seen a house with more than one bathroom. And what bathrooms they were: They looked to me like the ones in the films I watched on television. I was fifteen then, and that was when mother told me, wiping the beads of sweat from her forehead: We've both got to roll up our sleeves now, girl. My childhood was over.

Maria

Traveling in this taxi along the streets of this sunless city, I saw a display window filled with all sorts of bonbons, and it suddenly brought back the memory of when Mr. Karl caught me red-handed with my chocolate. That made me smile.

"And what are you laughing at?" Mrs. Anna snapped, her tone mocking.

"Oh, nothing," I said evasively, thinking how that woman was always watching my every move. "Just that—I like chocolate."

Mr. Mark looked at me for a moment and smiled. Mrs. Anna, when she saw her husband smiling, grew silent and stared out the window with a sour expression.

Mr. Karl usually spent the mornings at home and the evenings out. That was if no one came to visit him, obviously, or to practice, and then they would all play or sing in the piano room, and they'd close the door. Normally he would call out, Maria, we're not to be disturbed. Two months after arriving in Barcelona, he could already make himself understood. I don't know which language he spoke to me, but I understood him. And when he couldn't find a word, he would use body language.

After the violin incident, we had a silent period, a time when neither of us said more than was necessary. I did my work, and when I finished it, I retired to the kitchen or my room or I went for a walk. Until one day, when I had just gotten paid, I went to buy powdered chocolate, a bit of whipped cream, and some ladyfingers from the bakery. I sat in the kitchen to eat it all up. There was a café nearby where I often saw mothers taking their children for a snack. Sometimes there was also a maid there, but normally that was something mothers did, something they did with their kids. It was like a reward once a week or once a month. The children entered with their eyes gleaming, and they left with their faces all messy, and I was so envious.

I didn't dare go into the cafe and that was why I made a version for myself at home. And so, there I was with my mouth full of thick hot chocolate topped with whipped cream and scooped up on a ladyfinger that fell apart on my tongue, and I could hear the heavenly angels singing. I couldn't understand how that wasn't everyone's favorite food. Just then, with my eyes closed, I heard Mr. Karl's voice saying, I see you take good care of yourself. It still makes me laugh when I think about it, but I try to hold it in so Mrs. Anna doesn't get mad at me. That day I opened my eyes and found him standing there. I hadn't heard him come in; he'd been so quiet. I smelled something from the living room, and I thought you were up to something, so I tiptoed in, he told me later. Mr. Karl was like that occasionally: playful. And I couldn't think of anything else to say besides I bought it with my money. Then he started laughing.

I had never heard Mr. Karl laugh before, and it made me laugh to see him laugh, because he was so large and he laughed so hard that you couldn't help but join in. And I was choking with laughter, and he didn't stop, and I didn't know what to do. I finally managed to swallow the bite of ladyfinger and was able to laugh comfortably. And then he stopped abruptly and said, won't you offer me some. So I did, because I had just been thinking that I'd overdone it with the whipped cream, and there was plenty of chocolate to go around. Of course, I said, I'll bring it into the dining room. No, no, he said—and, to my surprise, he sat at the kitchen table with me, his legs spread wide on a stool, and waited for me to heat up the chocolate. He told me that he had only had thick hot chocolate like this once before, and that he'd liked it. Because in my country it's eaten in bonbons or bars and, anyway, not that often, he said in a somewhat sad tone.

Then, as he savored the chocolate, whipped cream, and ladyfingers, we shared a table and both took pleasure in one of the world's best combinations. He told me where he came from and what his city was like. He explained that they were putting up a wall that would divide the country in two, because people fled from one region to the other and they belonged to different sides. He had grown serious as he explained it, and I didn't dare ask who the two sides were. Recently, I had heard the news on the small kitchen radio where I listened to those afternoon radio serials I found so thrilling. And on the news they talked about that wall, but I didn't really get it; it had seemed so remote. And now it turned out that Mr. Karl was from there, because he was German and that I already knew. But I didn't know that he was from that place that was always on the news. I did ask him why they couldn't go from one side to the other; I didn't understand, since I could go anywhere in Barcelona and out of it as well, and to other countries if I had a passport. He sighed and said that he didn't understand it either, but that was just how it was. He also explained that in his neighborhood there was a square where he would meet with other musicians to play, a very pretty square. Even when it was cold, we would play, and that made us forget about everything, he said—and he smiled slightly as he spooned a bit of chocolate into his mouth. I didn't dare to say anything; I didn't want to interrupt those thoughts that seemed as sacred as a Sunday mass, and I could feel my heart beating faster because Mr. Karl was explaining them to me, and because it seemed that his thoughts had taken him out of my modest kitchen for a few seconds.

Yesterday, here in Berlin, I saw pieces of that wall they had been building as we shared hot chocolate for the first time. Over the course of my forty years with Mr. Karl, they'd had time to put it up and tear it down again. Yesterday I saw that Mr. Karl had been telling me the truth, that someone had built a wall cutting through the city—You see, Maria, Mr. Mark explained, I lived on one side and they wouldn't let me go over to the other side, only when part of the wall came down was I able to leave. And I looked at the piece of wall and I thought, *Well, it looks like it was solid enough to last for many more years.* And again I thought that I didn't understand why they didn't let people cross from one side to the other and vice versa. They had us all counted, said Mr. Mark softly. And then I thought I understood what the problem was: *If they switched sides, it would mess up their count.*

Teresa

Now comes that moment when the orchestra seems like a buzzing beehive because everyone is warming up at the same time. It made me think of my first attempts to play my violin from the dump. The neighbors were frantic, and Mother too. I had picked up the violin with sure hands. It must have hit hard when it fell into the pile of rubbish; the wood was peeled in one spot, but that didn't affect the sound. In fact, it sounded wonderful. Well, it sounded wonderful to me. My mother was sick of hearing it on the very first day, and the neighbors only held out a couple days more. They weren't the ones who had saved Mother years earlier; they were others with whom we only had a hello and goodbye relationship, and they knocked on the door to ask if I could, please, go out to the beach to play the violin. There the sound of the waves would drown it out. Forgive me, I muttered, mortified. And I grabbed the instrument and took their advice, I left the house and I went to the beach. We lived beside the sea, even though we couldn't even see it; the streets faced away from it and we never saw the sand or the water. The road leading there was filthy; that was where everyone threw their junk, the things they didn't use anymore but that were too big for the trash cans. Where are you going, girl? my mother asked. I didn't answer her; my throat was choked with tears as usual. I took my instrument and entered the beach along a narrow street, and leapt over all the obstacles between me and the sand. It must have been March; the day was cloudy, damp, and cold, but I didn't notice that. I breathed in the scent of salt water, of fish being brought in by the fishermen, who I heard coming in every morning, shouting. Soon I felt the wind mussing my hair and, gradually, as I drew closer to the water, I heard the sound of the waves coming and going—a sound that filled my ears and my thoughts. I set myself up right in that spot, because surely no one would hear me there. I put the violin on my shoulder, closed my eyes, and ran the bow along the strings, putting my fingers carefully on them. The sound that came out was bloodcurdling. I couldn't take it anymore. I broke out in sobs, put the violin down, and sat beside it with my head sunk into my arms. I felt like I was close to the music, but that it was just out of reach— that the door to that vast treasure was closed to me.

After a little while, I walked back home slowly. I dried my tears, and I told myself that it must be that some children were destined for one thing and other children destined for another. The girl in the book played the violin and I went through trash at the dump. And there was nothing that would change that.

I reached home with my heart broken into a million pieces. My mother was frightened: My girl, where have you been? What did you do? she asked me. She hugged me and covered me in kisses. I went to the beach to play where I wouldn't bother anyone, I simply said. She looked at me and saw the traces of my tears. Were you crying? she asked. Yes, I just can't find the music, I said, and I began crying again. And she hugged me again. At least I had a mother who hugged and kissed me. Maybe the girl in the book only had a violin and no mother.

Anna was like the girl in the book; she had a violin and no mother. The violin wasn't much, it was a beginner's violin, and one day I told Anna that she had to buy another one, a grownup's violin. I know, she said, impassive, curt, sarcastic. And that was it. She only broke her cool demeanor when she played, because she pursed her face in concentration. But then she went back to being herself: Anna the impenetrable, hard to understand and hard to interpret, an excellent and gifted student with a talent for playing fast passages at a lightning speed that I envied. But she didn't put her soul into it, only her intellect, and that was precisely how she had approached Bach—with her intellect.

When Anna turned eighteen, the maid stopped bringing her to class and she came alone. I already walked myself to school at seven, and it wasn't nearby. After the disappointment with the violin that day at the beach, I had been left empty. I didn't know what to do or what to pin my hopes on. I had never been drawn to dolls or toys, I was much more interested in the things we found at the dump—but after discovering the violin, it seemed I would never get that excited about any other find. And now I no longer felt I had the right to smile or to get my hopes up about anything.

But I should have remembered that the girl in the book didn't have a mother and I did. A few days later, at school, the music teacher sought me out—the one who would try to teach us to sing some songs to fill the musical requirement, in a time and place where there were much more pressing problems. She was a teacher no one ever paid any attention to, that teacher who went unnoticed and ended up giving us all a good grade in a subject that was so low on the totem pole that it was practically nonexistent. She came to see me with a smile and with eyes that invited hope. She sat down beside me, on a bench in the schoolyard, and said, I heard you have a violin; why don't you bring it in. Suddenly, the world opened up for me.

Anna

I keep running into that witch of a maid everywhere, and now I have to share a taxi with her. I made her sit between the violin and the door, but she never complains; she's so perfect. The perfect maid, of course. Now she looks at the store windows as if she'd never seen anything like them before; obviously you can't take her anywhere. But how could Mark even think to . . . And I bet she's going to start crying when we begin the concert. For the moment, I'm holding Mark's hand tightly, and I can tell that he is squeezing mine a little bit too, and smiling. Come on, Maria, I hope that now you can clearly see that there are some people who get what they want—and some, like you, who have nothing. And that Karl is already history.

The time for tears is over. When we found out he was dead, we all cried, and I felt as if they had amputated something deep inside me. A part of me was ripped out violently by his death, despite what had happened just two days before when I knocked on the door of his hotel room. But now I've lived with the hole for so long, and with the passing years it's finally gotten filled in.

Dark years pass slowly. Light ones, on the other hand, fly by; there's no way to catch them, you can't dilly-dally. It seems as if someone is saying come on, hurry up, hurry up, you're late.

Mama was always late. Goodbye, my girl, I'm leaving; ay, don't kiss me so much; you'll get my dress dirty, she'd say to me when I clung to her skirt to keep her at home. Ever since I can remember, I've always done that, begged her to stay. But she never stayed, like light years, like the ones that fly by. My mother was a fleeting flash, an intangible being, some sort of angel you can't touch or even be sure you've seen. You might have just imagined it. Take her to violin, she would order the maid. The violin was the excuse my parents had come up with to keep me out of their hair. Well, my father didn't even need one because he was worse than an angel, he was never around, you couldn't even catch a glimpse of him. Once I asked the maid if I had a father. Of course you have a father, Anna, she exclaimed in horror. And where is he? I asked, holding tightly to the hand of that woman I did see, who was the only one I saw at home, the only one who listened to me and also the only one who scolded me or called my attention to something I'd done wrong. Her name was Clara and she wasn't very pretty. When she took off her apron to leave the house, she put on this ghastly cologne. I told her not to wear it, that it stunk. I didn't hold back, making faces and batting at the air to get rid of a stench that made me sick.

Berlin is completely tranquil, but it hides its murky past in a river I need to visit again. My murky past was reflected, day in and day out, in the waters—not as clear and not as cold—of the small lake in the park we went through on the way to violin on Tuesday and Thursday afternoons. We heard the shrieks of kids like me, who were playing hide and seek or trying the patience of their maids. But I was going to class; I couldn't stay. One day, when I was dragging my feet more than usual, Clara explained to me that in the lake's water there were little fairies who stole the souls of children who dallied watching them. And that made me want to stay there even more. Come on, let's go, we're late, she said, pulling me gently but firmly. And I always missed seeing the little water fairies because of the violin.

I hated the violin.

Your father travels often, Clara would tell me. Your father has a lot of work. A lot of work, yes, but when he came, he greeted me just like all the other men who came by the house, and I couldn't tell which one was him. Until Mama said, sweetheart, give us some time alone. And she looked at me with big eyes, clear and pleading—eyes that said, if you don't leave I'll say something nasty to you in front of this man. Which one is my father? I asked the maid. And she described him to me. And it's because no one had taught me to say Papa to anyone. And saying Mama did me no good at all.

I had a small hole at the entrance to my stomach; it was always there, but when Mama left or kicked me out because she wanted to be alone with someone, the hole grew bigger. Then it was intolerable, like an ulcer that was eating me up from the inside. I had no way of stopping it; it just grew bigger and bigger. And, when Mama disappeared, when I saw her vanish, pretty and proud, through the front door, leaving me with the intoxicating scent of her delicate perfume, then I was torn apart completely. I stood clinging to

Clara's hand watching as the angel disappeared. At first I cried a lot, shouting Mama, Mama. Then I stopped because I realized it did me no good. I learned to pretend that nothing mattered to me, I taught myself to wear a gaze somewhere between languid and insolent while inside I was dying. I learned to keep up appearances. And gradually I became strong.

Maria

So it seems that in this concert they are going to sing some arias because Mr. Karl also directed opera. As I know full well. And I also know full well what happened the first time he directed one at the Liceu Opera House. Well, I don't know what went on at the Liceu because I didn't even consider going by there, but I do know what happened at home with that opera singer who almost cracked the plates with her shrieking. That was long before Mr. Mark showed up, when I had already gotten used to, over the years, opening up the large windows overlooking the park and watching nature spread its various seasonal colors depending on the time of year, hearing music in the background that Mr. Karl played locked up in his piano room—which I was only allowed to clean early in the morning while he had his breakfast, because later it was anyone's guess as to when he'd go in and come out of there. I no longer remembered my life before that; Andalusia was far in the past, as were the two or three houses where I had worked before meeting Mr. Karl. Of course, in the other homes I only had to clean, but with Mr. Karl

I had to do everything, everything that wasn't music. Go get these scores at such and such store, he would order, giving me a piece of paper with some names and I would say, yes, and head off. And I would also be sent to pick up violin strings, or call on the tuner when Mr. Karl needed him. I could tell when he was about to send me for the tuner, because the piano sounded very sad, like it was crying a little bit. Mr. Karl would also send me to pick up plane tickets from a travel agency where I made friends with the girl who sold them to me because she was very nice and always greeted me cheerfully, even though I think she did that because Mr. Karl bought a lot of plane tickets. And one day I asked her if she had ever been on a plane, and what it felt like to fly. She told me she had, and that you didn't feel anything, you just felt nauseous.

I didn't feel nauseous yesterday, but I did feel some very strange things. And I remembered that girl from the agency, who's not there anymore, because she turned into a woman and the years passed and finally she retired. I saw that last week when I went to pick up my ticket to come here. Everything had changed, and the agency too, after so many years, they'd renovated it, and it's much more light-filled and spacious. Then, when Mr. Karl started directing opera, he told me that it was very complicated and he would be gone more than usual, that he would be eating dinner at home less and that possibly a lot of people would come over to rehearse, so I had to be prepared.

And that was how it was: He disappeared for a while, he went through the door without even saying goodbye, not because he was rude but because he forgot to, and then he would show up again— sometimes alone and sometimes accompanied. And he would say that line: Maria, I don't want to be disturbed. And sometimes I would hear the voices of three or four people and other times, just one woman. But the times when there was only one woman's voice started happening more and more often.

The first time I heard that woman I thought she had a very pretty voice. When she spoke and laughed it sounded like the little bells we had in the dining room, the ones Mr. Karl used to ring for me. And then she would lock herself up with Mr. Karl inside the piano room and sing while he played. And then her voice wasn't so pretty. Then she screamed like a possessed woman, so high that I worried she'd lose her voice. The first day I was shocked, I was there in the entryway dusting the bust of Beethoven, who was the only one of those musicians that rang a bell with me, because his name came up so much and because Mr. Karl, every day when he walked by the bust, would say something that sounded like *gut'n Tag, Herr Beethoven,* as if it were alive.

Up close against Beethoven, trying to reach parts that were hard to get to with a normal dust rag like the one I had, I could hear what was going on inside the room quite well. Sometimes I would stand there on purpose and be swept up listening to the words or music or singing of those people who seemed like angels of the Lord, because they sounded as good as the organist at the church where I went to mass on Sunday mornings. And, well, there wasn't anything wrong with listening in, I didn't think it was bad or unbecoming or anything, nor did I think it was bad the day I heard the singer alone with Mr. Karl playing the piano. They were rehearsing a song with lyrics that sounded like Spanish but weren't. Lyrics that I thought I could understand, but I couldn't—and later, I found out that they were in Italian, which was really popular with the people who went to the Liceu. I was amazed by that voice because it was like one of those huge trucks that muffle all the other sounds on the street. What screams. And I didn't understand how they could come out of a human. My voice, when I sang *Linda paloma mia*, would be completely drowned out next to that one. I was so surprised by that sound, I found it so unearthly, that I decided to see how she did it, and I went over to the door, which had a keyhole that we didn't use. And I put my eye up to it and I saw them. Mr. Karl, his back to me, was playing as if his life depended on it, gesticulating with his entire body and moving his head up and down. The singer, fat and blonde, with a bosom trapped in a bra so big it looked like two frying pans, was also gesturing, but with her arms, as if she were acting on a stage. And she sang the whole song and ended with a shriek that I thought would break all the glassware.

And then something unbelievable happened. As I was getting up to leave, Mr. Karl stood up at the piano, went over to the singer and, to my surprise, he kissed her. He did it like in the movies, the ones they forgot to censor on television, because by that point we already had a TV and would watch it sometimes. From the other side of the door, my mouth dropped open; I covered it with my hand to stifle a gasp and I tried to leave. But I couldn't, no, what was happening in there was stronger than me—and when I saw that Mr. Karl pushed the singer onto the sofa, I thought that I had to leave, but that stronger force kept me stuck to the keyhole while in my head I asked God for forgiveness. He was always merciful with my weaknesses, and it would be a crime against decency to describe what I saw from that moment on, and a woman like me would never do such a thing.

Anna

Look at her, she's already been here for a while. Teresa is playing there alone, amid the other musicians, as if she were in the orchestra too. I hold tightly onto Mark's hand, until I'm quite sure that everyone has seen that there is something between us, something more than a professional conductor/violinist relationship. Pretty much everyone knows, but I want to make sure they all get the picture.

Maria is already sitting in the audience. She drags her feet, her head bowed, as if she is looking for a coin on the ground. That's typical of her class of people. It's so embarrassing to have to share a taxi and a hotel with her. Luckily, she isn't traveling with us. Look, I can't help it. It's mortifying, it makes me feel horrible; people should know their place and stay in it. Why did you invite the maid on this trip? I asked Mark, really surprised. Because she lived with him for many years, many more than I did, he answered. And that was that. Mark is stubborn and, when he's got an idea into his head, there's no getting it out. But taking a maid on tour with us, frankly, it's more than I can take.

But I didn't say anything more about it. Sometimes you can tell it's no use, and that's always been the case for me. The same thing happened when I tried to keep Teresa from coming. It did no good at all.

It had been a really long time since I'd seen Teresa. It was when I met her that everything changed. That was the end of the private violin lessons in that house filled with dark shelves lined with tidy scores in folders that smelled of dampness and poverty. That was the end of that odious walk through the park filled with children playing, to meet that hawk-nosed teacher who forced my fingers down onto the strings, *en souffrant,* as he called it, and he would press them down hard with his own fingers. It hurt, and I, who already hurt inside, hurt on the outside then, too. His eyes bore into mine, and one day he told me that I had a black cloud in them. Where? I asked him, flustered. Inside the pupil, he replied. And he pointed at it with a finger as crooked as his nose, and I blushed without knowing why, and I looked away. He pressed his fingers on mine again, hard against the strings, *en souffrant,* and I held back a cry of pain, and I tried to play mechanically. I tried to do everything mechanically, until one day he exploded and said to Clara: Tell this girl's parents that she's not cut out for the violin. Better yet, I'll call them myself.

And that day, when we got home, he had already called, and Mama slapped me. Again and again. Mama would occasionally slap me and leave my cheeks red, but that day they were bright as summer strawberries. Papa, when I finally figured out which one of those men he was, never did that. In fact, since he didn't even look at me, I had no interest in anything he might have had to say.

On the other hand, I was interested in Mama's slaps, because they felt good, those smacks felt like caresses, the caresses I had never been given, and now they were coming a bit hard, but they were finally contact between me and my mother—a touch that wasn't like the touch of a dress that would get sullied by tears if you got too close. I realized that Mama had become more irritable ever since the man who visited her most often had disappeared with a slam of the door. That very day, when I came near her, she screamed at me. Later, I provoked her and got a good slap, and the next day I thought to start singing in a very loud voice, so she would lose her patience and tell me to shut up and I would refuse to. That earned me another slap. And then it occurred to me to spill my milk onto my white Sunday dress at breakfast and I got two more. And on and on like that each day. I would seek out those smacks; I wanted them. But what are you doing, Anna? Why do you provoke her? Clara would ask me, horrified. And I didn't answer her; I just giggled, I found it funny. I'd found pleasure in those smacks, a pleasure that excited me more and more each day and encouraged me to be naughty. Mama's hand was warm, and a second after she hit me that warmth would spread, and for just a moment she would touch me, which was what I most wanted in the world.

The day of the violin, the last day of playing *en souffrant,* the smacks went on and on. I smiled as she hit me, and she did it more and more frantically because she couldn't stand that I was smiling—and, since I had realized that, I smiled more and held her gaze, impassive, aware of my strength in the face of her weakness, even though I was the one getting beat up. It hurt, but there came a moment in which I no longer felt the pain. I just looked at her

43

and experienced the infinite pleasure of her touch and that she was focused only on me, that I was the one exasperating her; I was the one who had her in that state. And I started to hear Clara shouting that's enough, ma'am, stop—and at first she ignored her, but finally Clara got between us and then, to my surprise, Mama began to cry.

Clara gestured for me to leave while she comforted Mama, and I obeyed and went to the bathroom. My cheeks were burning, my head was spinning, but I was still smiling. I swayed as I walked, like a roly-poly toy. When I reached the bathroom and looked in the mirror, I touched my cheeks. My mother had a ring that had turned and the precious stone had made me bleed. *En souffrant,* I thought. And, barely crying at all, I washed my face and then I dried it with a towel, taking pains to leave it really dirty.

Mark

She always finds me; she's always clinging. I can never be alone, not on the street and not even on stage like I am now. It feels as if I'm imprisoned, walled in again.

The day the wall fell, we all went out walking like automatons, and we didn't stop until we had reached the other side. Now it's hard for me to mentally reconstruct that wall that I'd grown sick of looking at—from a distance, of course, because getting close was dangerous. It was solid in every sense, with no holes through which to flee, as evidenced by the many failed attempts that ended in tragedy. For those of us who always dreamed of fleeing, those tragedies made our blood run cold in our veins.

And, suddenly, one day, there were holes through which to flee—holes filled with light, holes that led to freedom.

We were streams of people searching for one of those holes, a hole that finally connected us with the outside without the danger of death for trying to peek through. They had come looking for me the night before, and they had told me that it was all coming down—that you could get to the other side, that they weren't killing anyone, and they were shouting it. They were my classmates at the conservatory, and I was terribly frightened. I said shhh, they'll hear us, because in those days we never shouted; we said everything in a whisper, in silence. We couldn't raise our voices; we could only be discreet, paint discreetly and play discreetly—always beneath the attentive eye of the police who made it abundantly clear that we were not free. Ours was a silent country, a country of tiptoeing, a country where car engines were barely even heard. And then they were shouting, and they grabbed me by the shoulders and shook me: Mark, we're free, we can go to the West.

I didn't go that night because of my mother. She was very ill by that point and I couldn't leave her alone. She did live long enough to taste freedom, because the next day, when she found out, she got up, got dressed, and came over to me with shaky steps. Mother, what are you doing? I cried out, when I saw her in the hallway, dressed in street clothes and ready to go out. Come on, let's go, she said. And all that pain that she constantly carried, etched into her brow, seemed to melt a little bit, allowing a light to illuminate her forehead for a few hours—that light that came through that hole that had just been made in our enduring wall. I didn't try to dissuade her, I understood that she needed to experience it, that she didn't want to leave this world without knowing what was on the other side. The West Berlin that she knew was the Berlin destroyed by the war, by a war that she had been born into and that had forced her to grow up with the hardships of the postwar period. She had been born into prison and lived there all her life, and now she wanted to know what freedom was like. I want to see what's there, she said, grabbing her coat and heading toward the door. I followed her, I took her by the arm and we walked for a long while until we found the hole everyone was going through. And on the other side, freedom was shining. You are trembling, Son, she said, looking at me with a smile. It was true. I was trembling; I was terrified to leave there, I have always been afraid of the unknown, even when it is a synonym of freedom. For a while she was the strong one and I was weak.

Today, I can't believe how we lived in such a backward civilization for so long. But there is one thing I miss: the silence, the obligatory peace that forced us to put all our interest into what we really loved. There were no distractions, there was nothing that sidetracked us from our focus—which in my case was music. And in my neighborhood, the artists' neighborhood, we felt part of a special secret: the secret of knowing we were liberated by the art that came out of our instruments, or from the paint that filled our square with colors, or the clandestine pen that worked to disembowel the regime.

The sound of West Berlin was overwhelming, with all those cars passing by, faster than the wind. And the people didn't walk like those in East Berlin; they ran instead, they were rushing to who knows where. It seemed they were late for everything. And the West was all full of light, dazzling colorful light—with names of brands that I'd never heard of, which seemed further proof of the brilliant West that we had always seen, from the other side, as the best of worlds. Mother and I were mouths agape. Welcome, shouted some boys who came over with a bottle of wine and a few plastic cups. Mother and I drank with them, but soon they went to greet others who had come across like us. In fact, we moved forward impelled by a crowd of people. Of people who wanted to take on the world.

Let's go, Son, my mother then said. I looked at her and I realized that the pain etched onto her brow had returned. And it never went away; she took it with her to her grave. Surely, the effort involved in walking so far that day had accelerated the process of her illness, since she had little strength and had pulled it out of somewhere. When we got back home, I was carrying her; she couldn't do the last few meters on her own. Still, as I put her in bed, she found the energy to tell me, with a smile: I couldn't die without seeing it.

She died two days later. It was a month of death for some, a month of freedom for others. I buried her and then I thought about what I could do, if everyone was leaving home and looking to make a better life in the West. I thought of my father and I set off in search of him. I took my cello and my scores, I sold my piano and I landed in Barcelona on Christmas Eve.

Anna

"Let's get started!"

Mark taps the music stand with the baton. I get my violin in position. I haven't said hello to Teresa, haven't even looked at her. But I have tried to locate Maria—and after just a glance her way, I felt her eyes fix on mine. Her eyes have a supernatural shine to them. Maybe she's a witch. An evil witch in the audience and an evil bitch playing the violin beside me. But Mark is mine. And I want to take him to the river. I have to find my soul, and my soul is in the water, in water everywhere around the world, imprisoned there ever since the day it was carried off by the water in the lake near my house. Let's go there, I said to Mark this morning. You go, I have to rehearse, he grumbled. And now I have to go find the river all by myself and I don't know how. Maybe it, like Karl, has ceased to exist.

Karl was the first real man I ever met. My violin teacher with the hawk nose was more a woman than a man, Mama's friends were no more than bees buzzing around her, and I didn't really meet Papa until Mama left.

It was Teresa who opened the door to the larger world for me, when I started to study under her. Maybe you think that's the end of the violin for you, Mama said after that series of smacks, looking dangerously into my eyes—but now you'll go to the conservatory, and you won't get personal attention there; that's where everyone goes. Everyone means that's where the poor go, those who can't afford a good private teacher. I remained stock still as she spoke to me, impassive, holding her gaze to see if I would get a slap—but that day there were none. Oh, girl, you exasperate me; I don't understand how you turned out like this, she said with a sudden wave of her hand, and vanished on a pair of spike heels that I was very impressed by because I didn't know how she could walk on them. And then, that day, I don't know what happened to me, but something came from deep inside me, I was able to make out a latent crack in the inaccessible wall that was that woman whom I so loved and hated at the same time. And I went up to her from behind and I hugged her. And for a moment, for a brief moment, she stopped, and her heels stopped tapping—and, to my surprise, she stroked my hand. But it was just an instant, as if a moment of weakness, and then she said, not now, my girl—but without forcing me to let her go, just waiting for me to do so on my own. And, when I let her go, she left without even turning around.

I went back and found Clara watching the scene, crying.

Maria

First, the opera singer came out on stage. Miss Teresa and Miss Anna will play later. But now out comes this woman, not as blonde or fat as the one I saw on the sofa with Mr. Karl. When Mr. Mark indicates the entrance, and the orchestra has already played a few bars, she sings over it with a sweet voice—much more beautiful than that other singer—with a polished voice, with a voice that touches me where it should, some place inside where I have a sensitive string that can't resist this onrush; it shakes me up and tears me to bits, and there's nothing I can do about it.

In that moment, so many years ago, the first day the fat, blonde opera singer came over, when I pulled away from the keyhole, I decided to look for a boyfriend of my own to kiss me the way Mr. Karl kissed her. By the way, she came by the house a few more times and the scene on the sofa was repeated. It's worth mentioning that after one of those sofa scenes, Mr. Karl was very relaxed, as if a weight had been lifted from his shoulders. I should also say that I kept my eye out for that particular visitor—and, may God forgive me, I peered through the keyhole every time she came.

That was what made me think I needed to find a boyfriend. Since I only went out on Thursday evenings with a girlfriend who was also a local maid, it was no easy task. But finally he showed up on his own without my having to look for him. I mean that I didn't find him out with my friend but by going to mass. He was a young man who always kneeled at one of the last pews, like me—because that was a church for ladies and gentlemen, and those like me would keep to the back. I had noticed him before, because he seemed very lonely, but one Sunday he waited for me outside. It seems he had noticed me too, and when he saw me he said hello, what's your name? And I told him my name, and it turned out his was Pepe. It was one of those sunny winter days, and he was between me and the sun, and I couldn't really tell if he was smiling or what his expression was, but to me he looked a bit like another sun. We could take a walk, he suggested. And I said, okay. And that was how we started to date, and we went to the park with the lake and went around it a few times before I went home. He told me that he lived in a house close by—a very large house, with his parents who had been in service there for many years. And I always played with the children of the owners, he said, lifting his chin and acting important. And he pulled out a cigarette and asked me if I smoked. I didn't smoke, but I said yes. And I put the cigarette to my lips and I did what he was doing, which was inhaling the smoke. And I swear I almost died, because I started to cough and cough and I couldn't breathe. And he patted me on the back and told me with a smile: You don't have to smoke if you don't want to; it's not required. I got up from the bench we were on and, as I was still wiping away tears from the smoke and coughing, I said, I have to go. And he got up too and smiled and said: Let's meet next Sunday, all right. Yes, let's meet next Sunday. He was missing two teeth and I hadn't realized until he said goodbye. Those two missing teeth made me like him less, but I figured that wouldn't keep him from kissing me the way Mr. Karl kissed the opera singer. So I didn't think much of it.

Sundays were different from the other days of the week. Sundays were different because I always went to mass bright and early and because, when I returned, I always found Mr. Karl sitting on the sofa with his eyes closed and moving his arms as if conducting one of those songs that never end and have no words, one that I now know is called *Concerto for Two Violins* by someone named Bach, and his name is pronounced with a Spanish *j* at the end but softer. Mr. Karl taught the piece to me one day, but I already knew it by heart and had even added lyrics, lyrics that went like this, "Here I go, cleaning the house, cleaning up the whole house," and that kept me occupied while it played and I dusted the bust of Beethoven—his name I did know—and I said *gut'n Tag* to it just like Mr. Karl did, even though I didn't know what that meant. And I would sing, softly, as always. Then there was another part of the concerto that was slower, and it seemed like it was for dancing— and, since I had no partner, I put down the dust rag, picked up the broom and got started. And then the concerto would speed up again and I would go back to my singing. It went on like that ever since I made up the words. Every Sunday was the same, until one day, as was to be expected, Mr. Karl caught me in the act. I was spinning with the broom with my eyes closed, and going na-na-na and swaying as the melody continued. Suddenly, I tripped and fell to the floor with a little yelp. It turned out that I had tripped on

Mr. Karl's shoe as he drew near me. My temper flared, to his surprise—to mine too, of course. What are you doing? I exclaimed.
Be careful, man, didn't you see I had my eyes closed? As soon as
the words were out of my mouth, I realized I had stuck my foot
in it, and that I, a simple Maria, couldn't scold Mr. Karl just like
that—it should be the other way around. And I apologized right
away, turning redder than a beet. But Mr. Karl laughed, the way he
did when we shared hot chocolate in the kitchen and he got the
giggles. And he helped me up and said, come on, and he took me
to the piano room and sat me down on the bench. But what are
you doing, sir? I complained. Come on, Maria, you sing and dance
very well—you like music, don't you. Well, yes, but, I tried to say.
But nothing, he said, give me your hand. I gave him my right hand,
kind of embarrassed—it wasn't a manicured hand; it was a maid's
hand and not a lady's, and it smelled of bleach and disinfectant. But
he didn't mind and he took my fingers and somehow placed them
on the keys, and had me push with my thumb and he said: Do, as
a sound was heard. Then with another finger: Re, as another sound
came out. And mi, and fa, and sol. And that was all it took for me
to feel like all the fireflies I sometimes saw at night in the park
through the living room window had come to light up my brain,
and I felt my face grow damp with tears of joy I couldn't hold back.
Then Mr. Karl said, Maria, you are going to learn to play the piano.
I was shocked. He was already on his way out when I called out to
him: Sir. And he turned and said, what. And I said, but we won't
tell anyone. He smiled a little: Okay, we won't tell anyone. And he
left me there, wiping away my tears.

I dried other tears, the ones from my boyfriend's cigarette

smoke, on my way home. When I got there Mr. Karl had already finished listening to that Bach concerto. And I felt my heart sink a little. Then I saw him appear from behind the bust of Beethoven. You're late today, he said, tickled. Oh, I got caught up, I answered, turning so he wouldn't see me blush. What do you say, let's have a class, he said. What class? I blurted out. Piano class, he simply said. I was slow to react: Ah, okay, well sure. I followed him into the room as I took off my jacket with one hand and my hat with the other. Mr. Karl isn't rehearsing opera today? I asked, with ulterior motives. But he didn't seem to realize my motives and he just said, ah, that's over, now I have some concerts with the orchestra. I made no comment. I just let him teach me. Mr. Karl took up my fingers delicately, and then he had me do what he called a scale, from do to do—moving my thumb under the other fingers when I got to the end of the hand, because, obviously, that scale had eight notes and my hand had only five fingers, and the other three had to come from somewhere. And now the left, he would say, and we did it with my left. Up and down the scale, first with him helping me and then on my own. And next week we'll do it with both hands; just you wait, he said.

On that day I wished the lesson could continue. Going up and down like that, if you could do it fast, had to be a real surprise for anyone listening. Maybe it wasn't so hard to play the piano. Maybe even a Maria could do it.

That week a lot of important things happened. The first was that I learned, very gradually, to go up and down the scale with both hands. I was thrilled. It seemed incredible, and yet I was doing it. I was overcome with emotion as I went up and down the piano.

And Mr. Karl seemed very pleased too. He would clap and say, I think we've earned ourselves a hot chocolate with whipped cream.

The second thing that happened was that, at midweek, the doorbell rang and—when I opened it, the opera singer was there. I mean the one with the kisses and the sofa. Before I had time to say anything, she elbowed me out of the way and went straight to the piano room. She could hear that Mr. Karl was in there practicing his music. What do you think you're doing? I started to say. And Mr. Karl also started to say, What do you think? And here is where it all ended—because that day there was no kiss—instead there was one of those smacks that was so loud it echoed through the whole neighborhood. Mr. Karl was shocked. And the woman had the gall to say, before leaving: So you just wanted me for the opera. And she left with her head held high, wiping away a tear that I saw, even though she tried to hide it.

The third thing was that my boyfriend kissed me. He filled my mouth with the taste of smoke, a taste I wasn't sure I liked—but, after all, it was still the taste of a kiss like the one between Mr. Karl and the opera singer. I felt like he was sticking everything inside me, and I didn't know if I could breathe or not. And then he smiled at me with his two missing teeth and asked if I'd liked it. And I said yes, because there was nothing else I could say. And then he walked me home, wrapping his arm around my shoulders. And I slipped my arm around his waist. And when we got home he kissed me again before saying goodbye.

I opened the door and I found Mr. Karl there with a strange expression on his face, one I didn't know how to interpret. You have a boyfriend. I saw him through the window, he said. Yes, I answered, realizing that there was no way I could deny it. Mr. Karl passed by me before heading off to his bedroom, where he usually never went unless it was time for bed. And, before he disappeared up the stairs he looked at me and he said, because you are very pretty. Very.

As soon as he was gone, I ran to look at myself in the mirror. Having Mr. Karl say that to me was as if there'd been an earthquake and suddenly all the birds in the trees of that park had flown over to land on my head and all started chirping at the same time. I stared at myself for a while and, on that day, I found myself lovely too.

Anna

The first look from Mark at the start of the concert leaves me indifferent. But Karl's first look went straight to the depths of my eyes. It hurt, and it had been a long time since anyone had hurt me. Come in, he said in that strange language he spoke, a mix of equal parts Catalan, Spanish, and German. I followed him to a room where he had his piano. Along the way we passed Mark. He was nobody, just a boy who wasn't even thirty, who was still studying conducting and living off of his father's success. He said hello and disappeared. I didn't see Maria that day; she must have had it off, because when she was there you found her around every corner—like now, because that woman is like the plague.

Karl sat down at the piano and told me to play while he played the other violin's part, the one Teresa played, even though I didn't yet know that she was the one who would play it. That first day I pulled out my student violin, but another day, seeing that I could impress him, I brought the good one. A Stainer—how beautiful, he said, and a strange look passed over his face as if he had recognized something. Can I see it? he asked, and he took it from me and looked it over carefully. With one finger he touched the small stain that Teresa had explained was a crack that had been repaired, and he looked into the f-hole, and read the letters inside as if he wanted to be completely sure that it was really a Stainer.

But that was later on. The first day I went there, he stopped me right away. That's enough, he said suddenly, lifting his fingers off the keys. And he said to me, the other violinist had too much soul, and you don't have enough; where is yours? I was taken aback; no one had ever said that about my music. He looked at me differently and said, you play incredibly well—so well that it's scary. I felt myself growing inside. But then he continued: And yet you lack heart. Bach has no heart, I objected. Perhaps not, he replied, but he does have soul. And the violin does too. But you, on the other hand, you don't. There was a silence. I was deflated and thought that I'd already lost my chance at touring with that conductor, which had become my dream. Then he looked at me again and asked who had taken my soul. I don't know, I answered, shrugging my shoulders, unsure whether his question was serious.

But I did know. My soul left the day that Mama departed, never to return. One morning she was no longer there and I thought she'd gone on a trip, but Clara wouldn't stop crying rivers, and finally she said that Mama wouldn't be coming back. At first I didn't understand, but then Clara couldn't take it anymore and she told me that Mama had left a note for Papa saying that she was leaving because nobody loved her or needed her.

I left the house and went to the lake in the park. I was fourteen years old, and I no longer believed that there were little fairies in the water. But I did believe that the water, where pink water lilies floated on their wide leaves, carried off the little soul I had left—which, years later, Karl would ask after. Suddenly, I felt full of remorse, because I was sure that it was my fault Mama had left—because she must have thought that I didn't need her. And the tears I thought I no longer had in me appeared once again, and I spent the afternoon and evening sitting on a bench, crying. I emptied myself out—and the lake, which had sucked my soul, remained impassive, the way I used to do when Mama looked at me after hitting me. Perhaps it was faking it as I had.

At night, I slowly returned home. And then I met Papa.

Teresa

When Anna's mother left, she didn't tell me what had happened, but I saw that something was wrong, and after a few days, taking advantage of a moment when the girl had gone to the bathroom, her maid poked her head into the classroom and whispered to me. Now she's with her father, she explained. She's never talked about her father, I said. Because he was never around, but now he is; now he's here to stay.

My thoughts, current and past, always come wrapped in music, but now that I am here lit up and blinded by these spotlights, I feel as if, with Bach, all my life is suddenly well depicted. Bach is too exact, too clear. That moment with the maid was also very clear, and Anna immediately knew what we had been talking about. If you need anything, just ask, I said, realizing that the situation had become truly uncomfortable. Thank you, was all she said, and she brought her focus back onto her homework, onto the score that she had brought prepared for that day.

Anna was left motherless, and my own mother had grown old.

But before, long before, my mother had given me music; she had handed it to me on a silver tray. When that teacher told me, bring in the violin, let's see how it sounds, let's try to play something, I listened without saying a word—but the tears, my always sweet tears, dampened my face silently and without my consent. Oh, my girl, she said, wiping them away with her thumb, let's see if we have a little musician here—and she pointed to my heart as she said it. Yes, there was a musician in there, and she was me: I brought the violin into school the very next day. But first I came home and ran to hug my mother; I hugged her very tightly and cried even more. And she kissed me all over as she said, I so sorry I can't pay for a violin teacher for you. Maybe one day, sweetie, maybe one day.

It wasn't long. The music teacher was a pianist but knew where to place her fingers on the violin and how to press the first strings to make a sound as she ran the bow along them. And you say you found it at the dump, she said, admiring the find. Yes, I said, and it's a little bit cracked. I showed her the small line on the instrument. There are people who can fix that, she said, and made as if to grab the violin to take it away. I felt like I was dying; no, I shouted, no. Don't worry, I was just looking at it, she reassured me. And then she closed one eye and looked with the other into the f-hole, and I couldn't see her eyes but I saw that her lips moved as if she were speaking—but she wasn't, they just moved, as if she were reading something inside there, which I didn't yet understand, and that I now know simply means that the violin was a Stainer from 1672, a Stainer that I still can't explain how I let go the way I did. But anyway, at that time I didn't care that it was a Stainer any more than if it were a Sadurní. I could see the teacher's eyes as she let out a whistle and looked at me again in some sort of altered state. The expression on her face had changed when she told me: Don't lend it to anyone, all right? I nodded, but there was no real need for her to say that, because I wasn't planning on lending my instrument to anyone, and not because it was a Stainer but because it was a violin and it made music. And then she showed me how to make the same sounds she made on the piano with the violin, the whole scale that at the time I didn't even know was called the scale. And I went to the beach and practiced it. There, beside the waves, I made magic for the first time with that tool that was more than a violin, that was almost like the father I never had. I spent hours practicing the same thing. And the next day I stayed after class and showed the teacher how I was coming along. And she congratulated me. Then she found a score for me, of a very simple song, and above each note she wrote its name because I didn't know them. And she told me, when we meet a week from now you should know how to play this song. And I went back to the beach when I could, when I didn't have to go to the dump, and I practiced and practiced everything my teacher had told me. I ended up with cuts on my fingers from so much playing, but I couldn't care less, I didn't feel the pain, I only felt how, gradually, I was making a melody come out of that wooden box. I felt that I was managing to grasp the music, that I had it in my reach. After four or five weeks, the teacher took my mother aside and told her that she had nothing more to teach me, that I had to have violin classes. And she smiled and added another magical sentence: She will have a scholarship.

I went to the conservatory until I finished my violin certification, at the age of twenty. And two years later, I began working there as a teacher. With my salary, mother was able to stop cleaning other people's apartments and focus on her sewing. I also stopped cleaning apartments, and stopped ruining my hands. In my teens I spent my evenings worrying because I couldn't study what I needed to for the class the following morning or for an exam—and, when night fell, so as not to be a nuisance, I went back to the beach, as always, winter or summer. In winter I would cut off the fingertips of my gloves so I could play. And while I washed dishes in that home we had rented, I went over in my head the studies I had to play the next day. And when I was at the park with the kids or walking down the street or on the bus, I would do the fingering in my pockets to keep up my agility. I had to if I wanted to be a violinist. And that was surely what I wanted most in this world.

Anna

The orchestra's first violin is named Maties, like my father, like the father it turned out I did have. Mark stopped the concert for a moment to ask him to pick up his pace a bit. Maties nodded and the orchestra understood that they have to go faster.

At fourteen, I understood that everything had changed, everything. The day after Mama left, Papa showed up. He was one of the men who had come and gone, but never stayed for very long and never smiled at me or said anything. Wow, you sure have grown, he said, and that day he said it with a smile. And he looked at me with excitement in his eyes; where it came from I didn't know. Frankly, it seemed as if I had just conjured him up out of my imagination. Then, to my surprise, he asked me how it was going with the violin. Once I had recovered from my shock, I answered, fine, it's fine now. What do you mean? he asked, intrigued. We were in the dining room at home, so many years eating alone or in the kitchen with Clara, and now it turned out I had a dining companion, for breakfast, lunch, and dinner. I wasn't sure I liked that perfect stranger sitting down with me at the table like it was the most natural thing in the world, after a fourteen-year absence. But at that moment I felt obliged to answer, well, I didn't like the teacher I had before, but I like the one at the conservatory and now I like the violin too.

I said it like that because I didn't know how else to explain it. I didn't know how to say that at thirteen, when my gaze no longer wandered as I walked through the park, when I no longer had irrepressible desires to go play with those kids, I had discovered that an instrument, a violin, was the only thing I had, the only thing in my life that I truly possessed. For a while I thought I had Clara, but then she found a boyfriend and explained how she was getting married and leaving. She had explained it to Mama, and later, she explained it to Papa: If you'd like I can come by the hour, but I can't live here, she said. And Papa told her that there was no need, because it seems we had to have someone who was live-in.

So I only had the violin. Like now, when I play as if my life depended on it, playing at rebutting everything Teresa says to me with her violin and, sometimes, we look each other in the eye and it seems we're at war, in a war that began because of my father.

I remember that he leaned back with a piece of bread in his hand and rang the bell for Clara to bring out the dessert. And then he said, you know, it was my decision that you study violin, because it's my frustrated ambition. I wanted to play the violin, but, of course, it wasn't good enough for me. They made me study business management, you see, and we didn't have the money for more studies. You were studying with a teacher who was recommended to me and you didn't practice much, according to what your mother told me. But now you do practice, right? Oh, yes. What else could I tell him. So he was the one responsible for sending me to that hawk-nose violinist, *en souffrant* for who knows how many years. So he was the one guilty of my martyrdom. I hated him in silence. I drank a sip of water and retaliated: Why weren't you ever around? He didn't feel bad at all about the question, quite the opposite, it was as if I'd asked him the most normal question in the world. He looked toward the window and said, after thinking it over for a moment: Frankly, your mother was impossible to live with. *We agree on that,* I thought, but I stayed quiet because I saw that he wanted to go on. Clara brought dessert, and Papa kept talking anyway: I had to make my life, you know, just like she made hers, but we agreed that I would only come once a month for paperwork. I rented a place quite far from here, years ago. I told her and she didn't seem to care.

Inside me, there was a gut-wrenching voice that came from a bottomless hole, a voice that screamed: And what about me, why didn't you even say hi when you came, and why didn't you ever give me a single kiss, and why didn't you let me know that you were my father? The voice kept screaming, but only on the inside, I didn't say any of that out loud. Instead, I said something that I knew would hurt him, and I did it with a spoonful of cake in my mouth: I didn't know which of those men were my father, you see; I didn't even remember you.

I managed to hurt him, I could see it in his eyes and in how he stopped eating. I savored my victory over the enemy, him, as much as the cake I was swallowing. He didn't say anything more.

Later, I went out to look at the lake. The water was still and silent; it was the weekend, there were no kids, there was no one, except a couple of people walking their dogs. I looked at my soul laid out there, on the surface of the liquid medium that sustained the water lilies with all the calmness in the world. I saw it, my soul, and I saw it every day until it disappeared. It must have evaporated under the sun. And I thought that maybe, like the water, it would fall in the form of rain into a river, another lake, or the sea. From then on I look for it in every body of water I come across, and as I get close, I think I can hear it grumbling and complaining. But it only allows me to hear it, never to capture it.

That day, before my soul had evaporated, I went back home and said to my father: By the way, I need to buy a violin urgently; the one I have is for a little girl and it's very small. Papa smiled grudgingly but I didn't care, I thoroughly enjoyed the feeling of dragging him through the mud. You'll have your violin, he finally said, but we should talk to your teacher to find out exactly what type you need.

Mark

My father was truly obsessed by Bach's *Concerto for Two Violins*; my mother always told me that. It seems she would groan every Sunday when she woke up hearing it, early in the morning, and my father would be pretending to conduct with one hand, his eyes closed and in a state of ecstasy, as I would see him do in Barcelona, also on Sundays, always on the sofa, always with one hand in the air, always with his eyes closed. Sometimes, later in the day, my mother would tell me, he went out with his musician friends and they would improvise an evening of Bach in the square. He always, always played second violin, and another friend was the first violin, and whatever other musicians were there acted as a whole orchestra. It seems that, when they were young, after the war, in a time of great hardship, they played to distract themselves from their hunger. People came from all over Berlin to hear them, and my mother was one of those people there watching and listening to them, defying the cold, the hunger, and the state of emergency Berlin was in. It was an oasis of art and warmth, she would tell me. And that's how they met. He was starving, she explained with a smile, but he refused to be separated from his violin; he didn't want to sell it, he adored it. It was a Stainer like the one that Anna has. Hers was a gift, according to what she told me. My father had inherited his from an Austrian grandfather I'd never met.

Then my mother would tell me about the period when my father began to conduct his orchestra in East Berlin, which was when he started to make a name for himself. His dream was to conduct the double concerto with two female violinists he admired. Both of those women were already quite a bit older than him, but he was passionate about how they played; he said he just had to work with them before they retired. And he did; he toured all over East Germany with them and the orchestra, and that was what spread his fame over borders and walls. Of course, after studying that concerto for so long, I said to my mother, half joking, when she told me. And her lips tightened before murmuring, off-handedly, yes, and after studying them for so long. At the time I didn't know what she meant, but I didn't dare to ask. When he came back from that tour, she was waiting for him with packed bags. His bags. That was shortly before I was born. When I started to ask if I had a father, my mother explained that they'd gone their separate ways before I was born and that while my father may be a great musician, he was also a skirt chaser.

Today, about to begin my father's favorite piece, the Bach concerto, I wonder how my mother could really think that my father was interested in those women. I think my mother was just jealous that she couldn't give him what they gave him; she couldn't reach the musical ecstasy that he shared with his violinists. I say that because I know, because I find myself in the same boat—because I do have something more with Anna, but not with Teresa; that's just music. And that was something my mother never understood.

My father didn't just leave home. The regime wanted to promote him; he was one of their favorite musicians, and after taking him to the main capitals of the East, such as Saint Petersburg, Budapest, Prague, and Dresden, they sent him beyond, to the West. He toured the top European capitals and ended up in Barcelona with an offer to stay there. And that's what he did, convinced that he no longer had anyone on the other side of the Iron Curtain. He didn't know anything about me until I rang his doorbell that Christmas Eve, a month after the Berlin Wall fell.

Maria, the same Maria we met today in the hotel, who seemed not to understand why we'd brought her all this way, opened the door and found me standing there. She spoke what I took for a very odd Spanish dialect. I later found out that it was Andalusian sprinkled with Catalan. I understood very little of it at the time; I had only studied a little Spanish in high school. She was dressed like the chambermaids at the hotel near my house in Berlin, with a brown dress and a white apron. I had never seen anyone dressed like that in a private home, so I thought I had the wrong address. But I still said my father's name, and she gestured for me to wait a moment. After a little while he appeared at the door.

I look around. "Are we ready?" I ask, lifting the baton.

"One second, please . . ." says Teresa, adjusting her instrument on her shoulder.

I look at Anna out of the corner of my eye. She is ready; she's always ready, and she gets impatient with the others, especially with

Teresa. And then, when she is playing, she gets that wrinkle on her forehead, and her lips become more desirable than ever, more than when she smiled at me for the first time, more than when I saw her playing with my father and yearned to feel her close to me.

My father came to the door with a few strides. He cut an imposing figure, so tall and stocky. The woman in the uniform and apron had disappeared. I spoke to him in German, I told him right away that I came from East Berlin. He seemed interested and smiled widely as he invited me in. I followed him into a large room, with picture windows that overlooked a park filled with trees. He had me sit down and rang a little bell to call Maria. He asked me if I wanted a tea, and I said okay with a nod of my head because I was struck dumb by the luxury he lived in, which I was so unused to. And then, with the tea in front of me, he just said, go ahead, tell me, thinking that I had come with a message for him. What he wasn't expecting was that I would say I was his son. After a moment of shock, he asked me to repeat myself: What did you say? he asked. That you are my father. According to my mother, I was born shortly after you separated.

My father, the great orchestra conductor Karl T., was speechless. He must have been unsure whether I was telling the truth or was some sort of scam artist. I pulled my brand-new passport out of my pocket, and handed it to him. He took a look at it, and it said that I was his son. And that my last name was the same as his.

The great Karl T. was flabbergasted. Finally, he reacted, I'm going to call my—your mother. She's dead, I said, as he was already getting to his feet. He sat back down and didn't move, and I understood that he was in shock. That wasn't surprising, considering that in a matter of seconds, he had learned that his ex-wife was dead and that he had a twenty-eight-year-old son. I pulled a letter out of my pocket, the one my mother had written before she died. It explained everything. They occasionally spoke on the phone; he worried over her, but she had never spoken to him about me. In the letter she said that it was because she didn't want to lose her son. Given the political circumstances, if I went to the West, she would have never seen me again. My mother had put the letter into my hands shortly before she died: Go and bring it to him, she had said. And that was what I did.

Teresa seems be ready. I tap the music stand with the baton: "Let's go."

After the first moments of confusion, my father looked at me with those blue eyes my mother said I had inherited, and he said: It says here that you're a musician. Stay. And I stayed.

Maria

I close my eyes and let myself be carried off by the music, as if I were dusting off Beethoven. The music pierces my heart. The violin sounds so lovely, even though it is Mrs. Anna's. I can't help smiling a little; the Stainer sounds so good.

Look at the piano, Mr. Karl would tell me, because I was embarrassed to look at my hands there on the keys, with his guiding my fingers into the right placement. And now keep practicing, he would say; you have to work on it a little bit each day, do you understand? I nodded. Mister Karl would tell me that I had half an hour in the afternoons to play the piano and make music. Yes, sir, I said again, and continued doing scales, while he started to teach the notes: Do, re, mi, fa, sol, and he would ask me to do them out of order. Then he would ask me to give them with the corresponding sound, and I had to know exactly where the sound of the note was, because each had its own and you couldn't just make it up; there was one and just one. I tried it with varying success; there were days when Mr. Karl seemed to lose his patience with me—

but other days he would say: Very good, Maria, very good, and he would congratulate me. I felt so happy, as happy as when my boyfriend kissed me and put his arm around my shoulders as we walked down the street.

My boyfriend and I saw each other on Sunday mornings, always after mass, because he couldn't on Thursday evenings. And we were seeing each other for a year. At first he only kissed me. But later, one day, when we were sitting on a park bench, where no one could see us, he kissed me in a way he never had before—with a kiss that lasted a long time, and lit a fire inside me. It made him hold me tighter and tighter, and then he started to put his hand on my inner thigh, as if he wanted to touch me under my skirt. In spite of the fire I felt inside, I gave him a good slap and quickly said: What do you think you're doing? But Maria, he replied, that's what boyfriends and girlfriends do; you have to let me touch you. No, I said, not until we are married.

Thinking about that now brings a smile to my face. But at the time, what I was thinking of was Mr. Karl and the opera singer and the smack he'd received. I was unpleasantly surprised; I didn't expect that from my boyfriend, I don't know why. I already knew that some people did those things that Mr. Karl did, but I thought he was a decent boy. He was the only boyfriend I'd ever had, and up until then I'd enjoyed it—but that day I suddenly stood up and repeated: not until we're married. And I waited. I thought that he would say: Well then, let's get married, and that he would kneel down in front of me and ask me for my hand. I really thought that: I was such a fool; for heaven's sake! When you get older you realize all the stupid things you've done. Because that boy, that boyfriend of mine who sat in the back rows of the church, like I did, so it wouldn't look like we were trying to blend in with the gentlemen and ladies of the neighborhood—well, that boy, despite how much he devoutly prayed, found some other girl who would let him put his hand up her skirt, and maybe more. I found that out because, when he didn't show up at mass the next Sunday or the one after that, I got worried. When I went to his house, they told me he had gone out with his girlfriend. Of course, I thought that I was his girlfriend, and clearly I wasn't.

I walked back home with my heart hurting and my eyes filling with tears that I couldn't hold back. I looked at the ground, so no one would realize that I had just lost my heart's desire. When I got home, I couldn't see a thing because everything was water clouding my vision. I felt abandoned, betrayed, and alone, I had no one. I'd thought that I had the right to end up one of those women who marry and have children. And it turns out it was not to be. I opened the door and, without a word, without even a *gut'n Tag* to Beethoven, I headed straight to my room, stretched out on my bed and cried. I only cried for half an hour, and that was it—because I had to serve Mr. Karl his lunch, but my tears returned just as I had finished cooking and bringing him his food. I prayed: Dear Lord, don't let him notice, and he really didn't notice for a while. But finally he did. Yes, toward the end of the meal, when I brought out dessert, he said: Is the fruit going to taste salty today? I looked at the plate and a tear had fallen in one corner. Oh, sir, forgive me, I said, all flustered. And I went back to the kitchen to clean the fruit and put it on a new plate. Then, when I was in there, I heard his voice: I guess you and your boyfriend broke up. Mr. Karl was a direct person, and it made me cry even harder. I'm sorry, it just happened; I managed to get out between sobs. It happens to everybody, he said with a small smile. He was talking about the opera singer, I guess, and I blurted out: Oh, no, sir, it's not like that. I thought he was a decent guy and wanted to marry me. His reaction was immediate. Oh, fine, so you think that I'm not a decent guy. I was horrified: Oh, no, sir, forgive me; I didn't mean that, I just thought that, that . . . I didn't know how to explain myself. Then I lifted my head and saw that Mr. Karl was still smiling. It seemed he didn't mind too much what I had said; it seemed he even found it amusing. He stopped smiling for a moment to tell me, with a look in his eyes that I will never forget: True music has to be found down deep in the depths, you understand? I looked at him, now without tears, and I said: No, sir, I don't understand.

Mr. Karl didn't say anything, but that day he washed the fruit himself, and he told me to take the whole afternoon off—that we would figure it all out tomorrow. Thank you, I whispered. I told myself that, when all is said and done, I was lucky to have a boss who treated me as well as Mr. Karl did.

The next day he was waiting for me at breakfast time. I had managed to sleep and, despite my heartache, I was feeling better. Very well, Maria; we skipped class yesterday and we'll make it up today. I was about to say that I wasn't in the mood, but I couldn't because he came over to me and said: Now that you know exactly what the notes are and how they sound, tell me, do you want to continue playing the piano or do you want to learn to play the violin? He waited for my answer and I had to say something, so I said, the violin.

And that was how I began playing the violin, when I had already learned to do scales on the piano—and I knew exactly how the notes sounded and what flats and sharps were, and a few other things. Then, off-handedly, he said that he'd brought the violin that I'd thrown out from his walled country. That there he had inherited it from his father and that his father had gone to a place called Salz—something, I don't remember what—to buy it, a place surrounded by white mountains. White mountains and violins, he said with shining eyes. And they let me take it with me, because when you had such a valuable instrument, they would let you take it to the West to make an impression. I was shocked because I understood that the instrument was much more important to him than I'd realized, and I was the one who had thrown it into the trash. Bah, I barely remember that, it's been so many years, he said, patting my shoulder so firmly that I cried out. He never touched me, but that day he did and as hard as he could—and then he said: So, you want a hot chocolate? And there we were again, in the kitchen having hot chocolate with whipped cream. Mr. Karl was again laughing in that contagious way over something or another, and I really was heartbroken, but I was still laughing. I couldn't figure out how to interpret his strange behavior. When he came to the kitchen, he laughed—but when he left he turned into that serious, stiff guy who only knew how to play the piano, sing, conduct with his eyes closed, say *gut'n Tag* to Beethoven, and play the violin. This was the violin he bought after he'd lost the Stainer. When he left the kitchen, it was as if he turned into another person and disappeared into the world of music—one that was his and only his, and no one else could enter.

But those days were different. Those days, on the one hand, he came into the kitchen often and, on the other, he invited me to play the violin more. My fingers hurt from pressing the strings, but I liked trying to find the same note-sounds I had played on the piano. He didn't say anything more about the boyfriend who had dumped me or that stuff about finding music deep down in the depths that had left me so puzzled. But for a few days, he said more to me than he usually did. And I noticed it—that he was more present with me. Fifteen days had passed since things had ended with my boyfriend, and as I served his dinner, I said: I'm feeling better. And I added, thank you.

Anna

We humans are such idiots. We always fall into the same trap.

"Sorry," is all I say when I see that Mark has stopped the orchestra.

I messed up on a passage that I've been having trouble with.

"Let's go back," says my husband.

We go back and I realize that I'm blushing. I can't stand being the center of attention because of a mistake. I never make mistakes, but this time I was thinking about something else and wasn't paying enough attention. And I fell into the trap again.

I fell hard that time, too, perhaps because I needed to. I eventually forgave Papa for having disappeared during all my fourteen years of life—only because he came, he moved in and showered me with presents, and gave me everything I wanted. And also because he told me that we would take a trip, and we did—and because he told me that he would buy me a new violin, and he did. He had carefully listened to Teresa's explanations, he had gone to see her— to Clara's and my surprise. And I, who'd been so ashamed in front of my teacher for not having parents, felt good. I felt I could say, you see, I do have a father. In fact, I had swapped an invisible mother for a father with a real presence.

At the beginning, it didn't matter that Papa was there. I felt my mother's absence like a heartburn that was immune to every remedy. I was always waiting for her to come through the door: this woman who never even looked at me and gave me orders from up on her stiletto heels, who wouldn't let me hug her or even touch her. I was waiting to be able to enrage her somehow, so she would come over and hit me—so I could have that feeling of pleasure that I was unable to find any other way or in any other place.

That first night, when she left, when I came home after spending the evening at the lake in the park, I locked myself in my room. I didn't have dinner, because I thought that, if I ate, everything I swallowed would go down my throat into the bottomless hole and end up in my feet. I thought that my feet would get big and fat from all the undigested food. I stretched out on the bed and stared up at the ceiling of my room, where there was also water—because the park's lake was reflected and playfully swung back and forth up there when the window was open. Then it got dark, and I heard the crickets. I kept staring at the ceiling, my eyes and my heart dry. And I was without a soul, because I had given that up to the lake—and now the tadpoles must be eating it up. Then Clara came, opened the door, and sat down beside me. She was a maid, but she was all I had. I hugged her and I cried.

I would hug Papa some time later. I would hug him, and I would think, foolishly, that better days had come. I would consider Papa both a father and a mother—and, for a few years, I forgot that he hadn't been there for fourteen years, and he made me the happiest girl in the world. Until it all ended suddenly, because we should never trust those who show up late.

On the other hand, I had music, and I still do. I wanted to give up the violin, but Teresa had made me see everything differently. Even though Mama had told me that in the conservatory they wouldn't pay attention to me. She was so wrong. On the first day, Teresa asked me why I hated the violin so much, and I was shocked that she had noticed, that she could tell I couldn't stand to play it. I shrugged. Then she said, you have to hold it as if it were your beloved—like this. As she said, like this, she placed it gently on my shoulder. And now, you have to touch your beloved. My eyes grew wide as saucers. She joked, not like that, you have to touch his face and eyes and mouth to know what they're like, because you're blind. Close your eyes, like this. Very good. Now run the bow with an A. No, no—not like that. You aren't touching it; you are scratching at it. There'll be a time for scratching it, too—but for right now, you just have to touch it. Get to know it, like this; very good. Teresa spoke with a gentle, velvety voice—a voice like the sound that came out of the violin. It was a sound that I realized, from the very first day, had nothing to do with the sound I got out of it when I played with the hawk-nosed teacher. If your fingers hurt, take a little break, she said; you can't be suffering as you play. She looked into my eyes as she said: While you're playing, you have to make music.

And it turns out making music is easy. I only realized it with Teresa, after so many years of playing *en souffrant*. There was another path to reach the same destination. Why are you so nervous?

Calm down and relax; you'll never play anything like that.

Teresa told me magic words, Teresa taught me how to play, Teresa taught me to imagine. Teresa taught me everything. Later, when I switched from Mama to Papa, she must have noticed something. She said, completely naturally, that you could lose yourself inside music—distance yourself from the world outside. I'd never been told that before. The truth was that I couldn't distance myself from anything, but I did feel calmer as soon as I ran the bow over the instrument. With each passing day, I felt more that the violin was an extension of myself—as if it were some strange, magical growth. Then, when Papa talked to Teresa and bought me a new violin, I could tell that my life was starting to go more smoothly.

Papa was always home when I got back from school. He would ask me if I had a lot of homework, and would help me to complete what was due the next day. He also would ask me if I had any problems so that he could help to solve them. At first I wouldn't confide in him, but later, I did. He asked if I wanted to travel around Europe that summer, and I said yes. We spent a month traveling, and it was the best time of my life—even though I left my violin at home, I didn't miss it at all. When we came back on the plane, I thought that maybe I had been wrong—that the tadpoles in the lake hadn't eaten my soul after all.

I was sixteen years old when I first hugged my father. He had never forced me to; he could sense that I didn't want to get too close to him, because I didn't want what had happened with Mama to happen again. Inside me, I thought that the people we want to hug will one day or another slip away from us, and I couldn't bear the thought of living without him after we'd hugged. The day I did it, he hugged me back. I realized that he was crying, and he said: My girl, I never looked you in the face when I came here, because—if I had, I wouldn't have been able to leave without taking you with me. And your mother wouldn't have allowed that.

He was crying. I was, too. The world was kind, life was different. Everything was changing, happiness was here and lasted until I turned eighteen. I'd finished school and, with Teresa, I had reached my final violin studies with flying colors. Clara had gotten married, and now there was a new girl who spent the day at our house, but then went home to her own to live and sleep. At night it was just me and my father, and we were happy.

We were happy until we went to the Palau de la Música to hear a concert and bumped into Teresa there.

Maria

When Miss Teresa came to the house, I didn't think of her as a lady because I had seen her in the park some years earlier, and I'd seen her very differently than she was now. She wasn't a violinist or a musician or anything then; she took care of children in the park. She must have started the violin later in life, because then she was a young girl. But when she showed up at Mr. Karl's house, I said to myself: That's her, the same one. She wasn't dressed the same or anything like that. But I immediately said to myself, she's scrubbed floors and dusted just like me. In a way, seeing that Teresa had transformed into a lady spurred me on, and made me think that I could transform through music too. There couldn't be that big a difference between us; she must have been about twenty when I saw her working as a servant, and I had started with the piano scales at more or less the same age. I had noticed Teresa because the kids would get away from her. In those days, I would walk through the park at about the same time each afternoon, so I'd seen how she wasn't able to keep track of the two of them. I felt very evil, because it made me giggle, I found it funny. Poor girl, she didn't know how to call them to order—but I wouldn't have known how to either. I wouldn't have been able to keep them both in my sight. The whole kid thing wasn't for me—that's why I had rushed to work in a house where there was just a single man who didn't look like he was in any hurry to get married. The thing is, I saw Teresa the same way every day. It made me laugh, because it wasn't anything really bad. I could see that the kids were just playing at hiding, not being naughty or getting hurt. They did it just to drive her crazy. Then she would try to catch them, and I thought: *What long fingers, and what white hands.* I even thought they would be really good for playing the piano, because since I was already trying to play the piano I would look at everyone's hands and compare them to mine, then wonder if mine were long enough.

Teresa, Miss Teresa, came to the house after Mr. Mark had moved in. In fact, when Mr. Mark came, he would only stay there for stretches because he was also starting to tour all over the world. Before conducting, Mr. Mark played the cello—which captivated me the first time I heard it. I thought the sound was much deeper than the violin, and much thicker. It seemed that the violin was the son and the cello its father. While the violin reached every corner of the house, the cello's sound filled them all.

But who even remembers the cello now? Who remembers all those things in the past, those duets between father and son, those long evenings of music in which they discussed how each score should be played—and who remembers all the women.

I wish I didn't have to say it, but all that about getting down deep to the depths of the music seemed to be tied in with that.

With getting to the depths of the sofa. When a woman came in to play with him, I knew full well where she would end up—if not on the first day, then on the second. They would rehearse whatever it was they were working on—play for a long while, sometime hours, then they would talk and laugh. Then came the sofa. And I couldn't help looking through the keyhole, pretending I was dusting Beethoven, and saying *gut'n Tag* to him under my breath. All of the women who made music with him took their turn on the sofa—if they came alone, that is. A few resisted, but those were very few—and they did so with a giggle, and then never returned. But, in general, they were all like him; they must have wanted to get to the depths of the music.

This is a comfy spot, here in this plush seat listening to music. I could doze right off. Miss Teresa's violin thrilled. But not Miss Anna's. Mr. Karl had said it; she lacked soul.

One fine day, I stopped looking through the keyhole when the playing ended. Instead, I liked listening to the conversations about their craft that Mr. Karl had with the other musicians—both men and women. I was trying to soak up those words, so that I could one day play like them. After meeting Miss Teresa and hearing how she played, I was convinced that I could, over time, learn to play like all those people who discussed things that were starting to sound familiar to me—like the treble clef and the bass clef, and the demisemiquavers (a 32nd note), and the *anacrusis*, which was a term that Mr. Karl loved to use to refer to what part of the score we had to pick up from. I was already starting to play songs, and he gave me a book of songs from his country. They're easy, he told me, and very pretty. You'll see how much you enjoy playing them. I was so excited to see that book in my hands that I could barely hold it. It was filled with notes, and the best part was that I could read them. I could read them and felt I had the courage to give it a try. I can practice when you aren't here, if I have some time, I said—pointing with my head toward the violin. Up until then I had never done that. I didn't dare to pick up the violin when he wasn't around. He smiled: I expect no less, Maria.

And so it was. I practiced those songs in the silence of the empty house. They were sad songs that made you cry. They reminded me a little bit of *Linda paloma mia* and all those songs of mine that brought up tears. After learning a couple, I would close my eyes as I played them and imagine myself in front of an audience like the one that will be here tomorrow, with those spotlights that will illuminate Miss Teresa and Miss Anna, Mr. Mark, and the whole orchestra. And I imagined that they were clapping for me. But the best thing was that day when Mr. Karl heard me, when I played the song I had learned, and he gave me a few suggestions. But first he exclaimed, and I could see that it came from his heart: How delicate and in tune, Maria. He looked at me in such a way that I thought for a second, just a fleeting second, that Mr. Karl wanted to go to the depths of the music with me. Luckily, that look only lasted a few moments—then he started to correct me and tell me what I had to do to improve certain passages. I had my work cut out for me for the next week, in addition to the sweeping, mopping, dishwashing, and dusting, of course. I always had a lot of work to do.

And then came the best part. One day he was rehearsing with a singer and a pianist, and he called me in. I went into the room and said, as you wish, sir. He pointed to the sofa, the sofa of the scenes that I had watched through the keyhole. He said, sit down, Maria, and listen. Then give me your honest opinion. The singer and the pianist looked at me in surprise. They never expected a maid in uniform would be telling them what she thought of their music. But I had to obey Mr. Karl, and I couldn't help feeling proud that he'd ask me to do that—even though, of course, it was a very big commitment. So I sat on the edge of the sofa, because it didn't seem right for me to sit there as if I were a lady. And I folded my hands neatly over my apron. My hands looked nice, I had bought rubber gloves some time back and was taking good care of them with those creams I'd seen the ladies buy in the perfume store, because I didn't want Mr. Karl to give me another lecture about having my hands dirty with bleach and detergents. So the hands that now rested on my apron were the kind of hands that could be shown off. Otherwise, I looked the same as always—with my hair pulled back and some earrings I had bought when I'd saved up enough.

Mr. Karl conducted and the two musicians, after giving me an incredulous look, started to play. He closed his eyes and put his all into it as if he were before a large orchestra. The pianist played with enviable agility, moving around a lot. Her long hair kept covering her face when she swung her head. The high-pitched singer followed her as best he could, and pulled it off. His voice was lovely, but there was something about it that wasn't right—something that made it actually unpleasant to listen to. I recognized it right away, but I controlled myself well, remaining stock-still until Mr. Karl stopped them. Then he turned and said, Maria, inviting me to speak. Very good, I said hesitantly, because I didn't dare to say more. Mr. Karl looked at me impatiently: Come on, Maria, not compliments, what do you think? I felt lost, but I had to speak: Well, the gentleman sings, yes, very well—but it seems like he's not quite hitting the notes. I knew what I meant and Mr. Karl did too, but the singer got furious: What are you saying, what are you talking about, and why are you asking this? he said. Mr. Karl cut him off, turned and winked at me as he said: Thank you, Maria, you're dismissed. I left quickly. Then, of course, I stood behind the door and looked through the keyhole at what was happening. Obviously, the singer was telling Mr. Karl that he couldn't be expected to listen to a maid's opinion, and that he couldn't even understand what I had said. And then Mr. Karl answered with his typical calm: She was saying that you are singing below tone, just a touch. It's a question of coloring; it's very subtle, and I wanted to make sure, because I wasn't certain I was even hearing it myself, after so much rehearsal. All right, let's do it again. The singer didn't reply, and began singing again with the pianist with the swinging hair, who didn't seem to mind repeating the same fragment over and over— because boy, did they. It was no use; it kept coming out the same. But don't you hear that you are below the note? asked Mr. Karl, and he said no, that he was in perfect tune. In the end, they both got mad and decided to call it a day.

That evening, Mr. Karl thanked me and apologized for having put me in that position. It was very helpful, thank you, he said. Do you think that singer will get in tune? I asked. No, he won't, it's impossible, he said. He was recommended to me, but it's not working, I'll have to find someone else. Thank you, Maria. That second "thank you, Maria" meant I could go. I could already see that he was in a bad mood and flustered, and that I should leave him in peace. But from then on, he would sometimes call me in to hear his re-hearsals, and the musicians were shocked to see the uniformed maid sitting on the edge of the sofa listening to them play. Although, most times, when they finished I would say: You played wonderfully. Because it was true.

Teresa

Anna, the same Anna who is now playing with me, the same one who directs hatred at me every time she looks my way—a hatred you can smell, feel, and perceive; a hatred that shines in her eyes and she can't control; a hatred that she puts in her music now that she's playing with me—well, that very same Anna was the best student I've ever had. I realized that she had a special talent, even though she was missing something. She needed to put her heart, or her soul, as Karl would say, into it. Karl couldn't find that in her, because he had begun to doubt that she had a soul. First, it seemed she did, and I thought she really could become a first-rate violinist; her agility was exceptional, and in a violinist that's very important. There are very fast passages that most professionals struggle to play, and it turns out that she was able to play them in just her fourth year of studying the instrument.

The day that Anna came to class with her father, Maties, she was still very young. And I remember that she didn't know where to look, because the maid used to always bring her—then her

mother had left, and now her father, who apparently had never had any interest in the child, had shown up out of the blue. On that day, her father came over to ask me which instrument would be best for his daughter, because he wanted to buy her one. And Anna was looking first at the floor, then the window. I said to her, Anna, you'll play better with one for adults; you've outgrown this one. I said it to get her to look at us, but she wouldn't, she was eaten up by insecurity. She really had outgrown it and her mother had refused to buy her another one. Oh, she had no interest in music, Maties explained—and, in a low voice he'd added, but one of the conditions for her keeping the girl was that she study violin because, you know, I always wanted to play but we couldn't afford the lessons; my parents had enough problems paying for my obligatory studies—I mean, regular school, you understand.

Yes, I understood, he didn't need to tell me; I had a mother without a cent to her name who had scrubbed apartments. I wondered if he would also have scrubbed apartments to be able to study the violin, if he'd had to steal hours of sleep in order to do it all, and then practice for hours and hours. Would he have managed the snowballing hours the instrument and its professional study demanded, unable to take the violin to be repaired for several years, without the money to pay for even that trifle? I was always just breaking even, and my mother was having an increasingly hard time of it; she was very tired and very slow in her cleaning, so much that they finally fired her. Luckily, she still had her sewing, which she'd never given up, and she would sew and I would play, and we got by like that. I no longer played on the beach, though. I would play all morning long at home, but I played in tune, so I didn't drive

the neighbors nuts—even though I did repeat the same passages over and over to get them perfect. Mother, with her sewing machine by my side, seemed not to mind, even though I really did go on past the point of tiresome and was at it every single day. I only went to the beach when I was short on time and had to practice all night for something the next day.

We couldn't move to a new apartment, neighborhood, or situation until I managed to graduate—until I became a real violinist after passing the classes of instrument and harmony and composition and all those things you had to do back then, which are now a thousand times more. Then, the day I graduated, we went out to celebrate and we spent a little beyond our means on lunch. We had never been to a restaurant before that day, and we wanted to be served, which was what we always did at the houses where we worked, after all. That meant the end of looking for scholarships for my classes; from then on it was about finding someone to pay me.

In the first movement, Anna tries to best me any way she can. But now that we'd started the second, I'm beating her. The second, that *largo ma non tanto,* slow and drawn out, is where you need soul. That is where my gaze dares to meet hers, but she closes her eyes and brings her brows together to make that wrinkle between her eyes that I've seen all my life. It is a wrinkle I helped to create. And I really loved her; it makes me sad: She was an unlucky child no one had loved, even though it seemed that her father wanted to turn that around. Anna was my opposite: plenty of money and no love. But if I had to choose, I'd stick with my childhood, full of love but no money.

I found work right away; they were looking for new teachers

at the conservatory and it was a time of change. The dictator's regime fell and everything was different. Everyone was protesting over everything, and I just wanted a job. I got one and I didn't leave there until I had to ask for a leave of absence to go on tour with Karl. And then other conductors started to ask me to play for them. My life took a turn with the change of the century. Everything is change, like Karl's East Berlin, which despite everything is still run through with some scars, traces of a wall that separated people without any criteria. Just because some lived here and others there, they weren't allowed to cross to the other side. I know Mark quite well, and he also carries that scar, in his eyes. And Karl had it too.

And when I saw my mother for the last time, she had generosity in her eyes. Now that we live well, she said with resignation. Those were her last words, and she was right. We were living in the new apartment, I had been a teacher for a few years, and Anna had already been my student for about one. I missed two days of class and, when I returned, I told all the students what had happened, and they all gave me their condolences. But not Anna, Anna didn't say a thing. And I looked at her and realized that her gaze was hostile, that she was recriminating me for not having gone to class, for having missed my student-teacher date with her; she didn't find it right at all that I hadn't been there. The truth is that in that moment I found it strange, but then I forgot all about it when life went back to normal, and our student-teacher relationship did as well.

But I saw that same look in her eyes when Maties and I started to date. I had bumped into Anna with her father at the Palau de la

Música and that was where it all started; we began chatting. Years had passed and Anna was very far along in her studies, she was a girl who, bit by bit, had learned happiness and sensitivity at her father's side, and musically she had come a long way as well. She had relaxed and managed to do what it takes to make music, real music.

But it didn't last long, because that was the end of it all. We all went out to dinner and she seemed happy, but then Maties and I exchanged phone numbers and she didn't like that as much. When she realized that something special was growing between us, she changed again and, suddenly, I saw in her the girl who met me with hostility when I returned to class after burying my mother. That day she was afraid of being left by the only person who was there for her. And then, with Maties, she thought I was snatching her father away from her.

Maybe we should forget about this, I sadly said one day to Maties, when I thought the situation was untenable. No, she will understand; she has to understand, he said. After all, he was right, a girl who was already an adult couldn't dictate what her father did with his life. But it hurt me, and suddenly, Anna stopped putting what she had been putting into her music. It was as if it were all tied together: her personality, her moods, and, above all, her soul. Suddenly, she had lost it again, and no matter what instructions I gave, there was no way to get her back to the Anna she had been before, the Anna of the past four years. I tried to talk to her; I asked her if she was upset by the fact that her father and I were dating. She answered that our lives weren't her business, although she wouldn't meet my gaze, and she asked me to go back to the music:

that we didn't have much time, all of a sudden she was always in a hurry, she always had to leave.

My relationship with Maties grew, while my relationship with Anna deteriorated. When I went to their house, she was never there, or she disappeared as soon as she heard me come in. She had become invisible. Then, at the conservatory, they told me she had requested a different teacher. I was shocked.

Then I did what I never should have done, but it was a last ditch attempt to get her on my side, to get her to at least have a bit of affection for me. For all three of our sakes, I gave her my Stainer. She had seen it on more than one occasion, and I knew she envied it. I had never told her where I'd gotten it; normally, I taught with another violin and only brought it in every once in a while. And then I gave it to her. I thought that that would solve everything, that letting go of a gem like that was worth it if it meant winning over a person I needed on my side. I also thought that things with Maties would move forward and that we'd eventually end up living together, and the violin would stay in the family. I don't know what I was thinking, but I gave it to her.

That day when I lost my head, I also lost what had saved my life at the age of seven. I didn't get anything out of it, except for a thank-you and a sarcastic smile. At our last class, I placed it gently in her hands. Since it was a magic violin, I thought that it would allow Anna to find her soul in music. But that wasn't the case: in her hands, the Stainer turned into just another instrument, nothing more, it no longer made magical music, it lost its enchanted aura I had seen at the dump. But she didn't refuse to accept it, she took it immediately. I was left without Anna, without the violin, and, a few years later, without Maties as well.

Now, she pulls the Stainer out as often as she can in front of me, to rub my nose in it, and I think I'll never find another like it. Giving it to her was so stupid of me—so, so stupid. But Anna is the one who lacks true music, with or without the Stainer. And I've got it.

Anna

This second movement is for sappy, sluggish people like Teresa. It's too easy for me. Sure, it's pretty, and Teresa goes wild for that kind of thing; you can see it a mile off, it looks like she's about to burst into tears. I won't look at her now, I'll wait until the last movement, when it speeds up again, when I can fly while she just hops along trying to keep up. I don't understand what Karl saw in her, I don't understand what so many conductors see. Playing the violin has been a race since Vivaldi's time, and anyone who thinks otherwise isn't meant for this instrument.

Teresa wasn't meant for Papa, and Papa wasn't meant for Teresa. That's why their relationship ended the way it did, suddenly. Things that don't work, end; that's obvious. And, sometimes, the ones that do work end too, because the relationship between me and my father did work. During a simple part of my life, for a few years, it was as if I wasn't myself because I was living atop a cloud; it was as if the sky had opened up just for me, after so long living without a mother and without anything, without anyone, just Clara. Papa explained with tears in his eyes how he couldn't be there for me, that Mama had said either you or I, and didn't even want him to see me. And, as he had already told me on other occasions, he preferred it that way, not seeing me, because if he had he wouldn't have been able to stand leaving me there with her. He had told me that so many times and asked for my forgiveness so many times that, in the end, one day a spurt of water came up from inside me, one I couldn't keep from traveling up through my neck. I broke out into tears and that was when I hugged him close and told him that I had never been able to do that with Mama. I don't know why I fell in love with her, he told me, she wasn't all there; all she did was flitter about from one party to the next and from one lover to the next. I was one of many, but I wanted to think it was something different, I believed that for a while. And he would look at me with those damp eyes and say, forgive me, please.

And then it was like the first movement of this concerto, a joy that ran through my body every day as I got out of bed, that sent me to school and to violin and harmony lessons with a smile on my face, a smile I'd never worn before. My goodness, Teresa would say, you have a very pretty smile. You have a lovely smile.

Tomorrow, come hell or high water, I have to see the Spree. Maybe that's where my soul has ended up. Ten years ago it seemed that it was escaping into that very river. Mark has no time for anything, he says, he's always rehearsing; that's what comes with being the conductor. And I can't help being drawn in by the water, in a way that nothing else draws me in, except for the feeling of vertigo that takes hold of me when I play the Baroque composers so fast; I can't resist it. But apart from that, nothing draws me in the way water does, and every-where I go I have to visit the water, if there is any; it's like a courtesy visit to my own soul, because I feel it, I sense its presence, and I think: Perhaps today it will come back to me, and then I say hello, how are you, dear, and my taciturn soul stays quiet, silent, keeping me from knowing where it is exactly—so I don't catch it unaware and take it with me. And, I really hate when, while I'm looking for it, someone comes over to play with the water, skipping stones or setting off a toy boat or sailing by. At which point I'd like to say, hey, where do you get off talking to my soul; it's mine and mine alone, you go talk to yours, if you have one. But I can't say anything. Sometimes I've found people staring because, without realizing it, I've spent ten minutes looking at one point on the pond, river, or lake. Not the sea, which I never visit because the motion of the waves wears me out, and I'm quite sure my soul isn't there.

But I have to find it, because I can't live without a soul.

The day I realized that there was something between Teresa and Papa, my world fell apart. I wanted to go find Teresa and scream that Papa was mine, that she and her Stainer needed to back off, leave, and never come back. I couldn't stand the way she looked at me, somewhere between tender and compassionate, which is to say that for some years she was a comfort, I'll admit that; Teresa was more than a violin teacher, she was a support for me, and even though we spoke little of subjects other than the violin, I knew that I was her favorite student and I even thought she loved me.

And then, when she took Papa from me, she showed her true self. They started to meet up, seeing each other both in and out of the house, and I didn't want to know anything more about it; I made sure to leave before she came over. Suddenly, Papa wasn't there for me the way he had been, he wasn't around, he disappeared for entire weekends, and when he returned, his mind was on dates with Teresa and waiting for the phone to ring, and luckily, social media didn't exist yet, because otherwise he would have spent his nights chatting online the way teenagers do now. And when he was with me, he seemed to be in another world, and sometimes he would drift off when I was talking to him, and I'd realize that he wasn't listening.

My world fell apart, it really did. I had given him what I'd never given anyone, and he had taken it and made me believe that he was going to give me his all in return. And it turns out that that wasn't the case, that he hadn't given me anything, he had just tricked me. I felt as if I had been torn in two, Papa had been with me when he didn't have anyone else, but now that he'd found Teresa, I meant nothing to him; I was just a bother he was forced to put up with, that was painfully clear.

I spent my days playing the violin and looking at the lake. I spend hours just staring into it. And I put in a request at the conservatory for a change of teacher, because I couldn't bear being around Teresa and I couldn't stand her correcting me or telling me what to do. What I did like was turning my back on her when she feigned interest in me, and she would make a pathetic face, as if she couldn't live without that smile of mine that she'd been so fond of. And I enjoyed making her suffer, that was my only joy, and I loved thinking that she would burst into tears when I left the classroom. I got her so distraught that, on our last day of class together, she gave me her Stainer, which now I flaunt in front of her every chance I get. It goes without saying that her gift was the confirmation of my victory over the enemy. All I said was a polite thank you. Now I had totally beaten her, I'd left her with nothing, just Papa, there was no way to snatch him from her clutches, and I thought, *Why don't you leave him, if you love me so much, don't you realize you've taken from me the only thing I've ever had?* But no, she realized nothing, she gave me everything except for the only thing I really wanted: Papa.

After some time, when I no longer studied with Teresa, Papa finally reacted. I mean that his initial infatuation with her passed and he remembered my existence. He sat me down to have a talk. He told me that I'd been acting strangely, that it seemed I didn't like his relationship with Teresa and he wanted to know why, when he thought my former teacher and I got along so well. First, I was evasive and did my best to change the subject. But then, since he kept insisting, I broke down, shouting and crying, I told him that he didn't pay any attention to me, that he didn't listen to me, that he wasn't there for me, that he only talked about her and only wanted to be with her. I let it all out in a rush, and I think he was a bit shocked. Maybe he wasn't expecting that. He came over to me, said something like one thing didn't cancel out the other, that he loved me very much, and he tried to hug me like he used to. And I was dying for his hug, but I didn't want him to do it because if he did, I would dissolve into tears in his arms and he would console me and the next day he would return to Teresa and we'd be back where we started, and I would have hurt myself, because these things hurt a lot and sometimes it seems no one realizes that. So I told him to leave me alone, and I left him there with mouth hanging open.

Every time I look at the maid, sitting there in the concert hall, I have the feeling that her eyes are drilling into my brain. And she's just a maid who's dying of old age anyway, and I don't know what it is about her, but her gaze makes me nervous.

Papa didn't come near me for a couple of days. Finally, on the third day, he came over with his eyes gleaming and some airplane tickets in his hand. Look, he said, let's you and I go on a trip together alone, for a whole week, how does that sound? Then I was the one surprised, I hadn't expected that. The idea was very tempting, the possibility of having my father to myself for a week. On the other hand, if I did that, the inevitable return would be terrible, we'd be back to square one, I didn't trust him or anyone anymore. Where? I asked to buy some time to think. To Monte Carlo, he said. Look, here are the tickets, and we'll rent a car when we get there, what do you think?

We went. I was filled with contradictory feelings like hatred and desperate love that began and ended with that man who was everything to me. It wasn't like it'd been before, not even close— but it could have been, in time, if we'd continued in that vein; he was sweet and affectionate with me, and I didn't see him call Teresa even once.

But I didn't trust it; I knew full well that it would all end as soon as we got back to Barcelona. Papa only wanted to patch things up with me, probably just to ease his conscience. And I would be alone again. I couldn't stand being alone anymore. Life was over for me, there was nothing that made me feel alive, not even the violin and the fastest passages by Vivaldi, Bach, and Veracini. It was all over, everything.

One night during that week, at the casino, I drank too much, on purpose. Papa didn't realize, he was busy gambling. When we left, I pretended to be sober, and I asked if I could drive us to the hotel. I had just gotten my license and was always asking him to let me use his car, so he didn't see anything strange in my request. He sat shotgun and started chatting about his bets, how he'd done. I stepped on the accelerator. I remember that he warned me about speeding on a winding highway beside the sea. I remember wanting to go headfirst off the cliff and drown us both in the sea, so Papa would never again belong to Teresa. And that's it, I don't remember anything more.

Mark

Third movement. I look at the orchestra and I look at my violinists. Anna and I understand each other perfectly. I know that Teresa had that with my father. He always kept his distance except where music was concerned. I think that, for him, each concert or opera was like a love affair with his soloist or star singer. He enjoyed working with women, it was curious how he always managed to get everything to sound better when he worked with women.

Sometimes I wonder if he ever touched Maria, I mean if he tried to get involved with her. I don't think my father was like that, and now it's impossible to imagine, with him dead and her so old that I'm not even sure she'll survive the trip back home alone, because she insisted on traveling by herself. It seems she has family here, even though she hasn't introduced them to us. She must be embarrassed, thinking we'd have nothing in common.

Maria and my father spent many years alone together in that house, until I showed up. Maybe there was something between them, I don't know. Either way, when I arrived in Barcelona, luckily

I had Maria to help me with the day-to-day stuff, because my father always had his head in the clouds and if I had to rely on him I would have run into problems everywhere. That strange, cosmopolitan city was filled with danger for a man like me who was used to a routine that included the security and tranquility of knowing that everything was in order. Because that's how it was on the other side of the wall: You didn't have to worry about a thing, there were no complicated or different situations, everything was always the same, it was like a *tout compris* trip; I always had food and clothes to wear. If I wanted to choose what I ate or wore, then things got more complicated. One of my mother's cousins, who lived in West Berlin, would sometimes manage to bring us some of the clothes we saw on TV. I didn't care how I dressed, but it made my mother happy. And there was also the color television that same cousin brought for Christmas one of my last years there. Our neighbors were shocked and dying of envy.

It's odd because now I'm in Berlin, and yet when I think of the city I grew up in, I think of a different city, when really it's right here, on the other side of a wall that no longer exists. I've played concerts in the Staatsoper that is now being renovated, and I remember the front rows filled with military men. But this place isn't the one I remember, not by a long shot.

Where are you going with that, Mr. Mark? Maria would scold, because I carried around a radio cassette player: Don't you see they'll steal it, you'll be mugged in some of the rougher neighborhoods? I was surprised, and she rushed to give me a bag to keep it in. And when the bus didn't come, I didn't know what to do, and I would be late for rehearsal, because in the East, when the bus didn't come, everybody was just late for wherever they were going, but in Barcelona, when I explained that I was late because of the bus, they said I should have taken a taxi, and I would say that the idea hadn't occurred to me. One day I was mugged, and another time my pocket was picked on the Ramblas while I watched some jugglers. You are a bit naïve, Maria would laugh, fresh off the boat, like a kid with no sense of direction, Mr. Mark.

Please, don't call me Mr. Mark, I begged her for the millionth time. Oh, yeah, she said, tapping her head, forgive me, Mark, force of habit. Then, when she would do it again, I answered yes, Miss Maria, and that would make her realize she'd slipped the Mr. in again.

Maria managed to keep the house neat and in order, always to her taste, of course, because as far as domestic subjects were concerned, it was as if my father didn't exist. But Maria was something more, I don't know what; she had a special touch that I could never put my finger on exactly. It must be that same sensitivity that has her sitting out there now, watching the musicians with an almost sacred concentration. Maria is a special woman.

Teresa

Every time I look into Anna's eyes, I remember her gaze and the last words she said to me in the hospital. They shook me up so deeply that it took me a long time to recover.

We are always slow to recover from a true wound. And I wasn't prepared for that, not in the slightest. When they called to tell me, I felt my world crumbling. They did it the way they do, we're sorry to have to give you bad news, it seems Maties had my phone number somewhere on him, the girl is seriously injured, and he didn't make it. They say he didn't make it, and you don't know what to do with yourself. You ask what happened, and they say an accident, it's a miracle they didn't end up in the sea because there was a bit of beach below, and the girl survived, for the moment, they say, because they always play it safe, they don't make any promises, in case the girl also ends up dying when they'd said she'd pull through. They said that she was driving, that she'd been drinking. And then you think, *Poor girl, with all those inner conflicts she had, it's no surprise,* and God knows what else you think as you grab your jacket

117

and rush out of the house and toward the hospital. Does the girl have a mother? they ask you. Yes, but she left her, she's gone, you explain, not knowing if you've said too much. And you think that now it's up to you to be her mother.

I arrived at the hospital with my heart aching over my tragic loss. She is in the ICU, there are visiting hours, they said, and you aren't family. She has no one else, I explained a bit curtly, except for the servants, and her father and I were involved. Oh, okay. Then they lowered their voices to say, I'm so sorry, they were referring to Maties, and my insides turned to jelly, and I felt myself floating in a sea of tears, and then they led me to that monitored bed where she lay unconscious surrounded by nurses and security measures, in case her heart or some other organ failed and they'd all have to come running. You have ten minutes, they told me, and I held her hand. She didn't open her eyes the first day, and then later, when she opened them she couldn't talk, she had tubes coming out of everywhere, including her mouth, and the tears flowed from her eyes only because there was no machine to keep her from doing that. And I would say to her, don't cry, and I would take her hand in mine and I could feel her squeezing and I thought that things would change between us from then on, sadly because of the death of the man we both loved most in the world.

The two of them taking a trip together had been my idea. I think she feels you aren't there for her anymore, I had said to Maties, worried by his daughter's attitude. And I added, it might be a good idea for you two to go somewhere for a few days, that way she'll see that nothing has changed and you love her the same as ever. It sounded like a good idea to Maties, and they took the trip. I don't know how it went, I told him he didn't need to call me, that it would be best if she didn't see us talking, it'd be better if he focused all his attention on her. And I waited, trusting that it would all work out.

We are too trusting. Time has passed and she hasn't changed. Fortunately, I have. And now Anna is an adult, now she has Mark and doesn't need anything more. Maybe she's finally found what she was searching for.

There in the ICU, I wiped away her tears with the tip of a handkerchief, with the only dry corner I had left after drying my own tears, over losing the love of my life. I'd flirted with the occasional fellow teacher, but it had never gone past that. And then when I had found Maties, I'd lost him. As I haunted the hospital hallways, waiting for visiting hours to start so I could see Anna, because I didn't want to miss a single day, I didn't want her to feel alone if I could be with her; I wondered how I would tell her that she had lost her father, when the time came to do so. I can do it, I told the nurses. But not yet, they replied, you have to wait until she's out of intensive care; it is a risk to her recovery right now. I obeyed, when you're in a hospital you always obey the nurses, and that gives you the feeling that someone knows what is going on and is concerned for your grief. Later, when you've left the hospital, you miss that kindness that's inevitably habit-forming, because you feel bundled up in pillows at all times, surrounded by the smell of different medicines that you can't get out of your nose, but which inexplicably, on your first days out, you think you even miss.

And I waited for Anna to be out in the regular ward. That move out of intensive care is, in a hospital, like graduating, like getting your basic diploma: Okay, now you can continue with your college prep. You haven't finished school, but you've gotten your first certificate so you can go out in the world and get a job and prove that you're good for something.

The day they told me that Anna was out of the ICU, I was so thrilled. I went running up the stairs; that was great news, even though next came the worst part, having to tell her about her father's death. I went into her room. Anna was a bit broken everywhere, but the danger of internal hemorrhaging had been resolved, and she lay in a white bed in a room for two. She no longer had tubes coming out of her, just the serum that went into a vein through a needle they'd stuck into her hand. And one leg in the air, and one arm in a cast. In the other bed, another girl with a leg in a cast was flipping through a magazine.

I went over to Anna's bed, with my back to the other girl for a bit of privacy. She looked at me as if she'd never seen me before. There was a mix of incredulousness and hatred on her face. What are you doing here? she asked. I was a bit shocked but finally answered, I've been with you in the ICU all these days, don't you remember? No, she said curtly. At first I was surprised, but then I recalled that no one ever remembers anything about the intensive care unit; God knows what they put into your blood to make you forget everything. So then I screwed up my courage to tell her, as gently as I could and fighting back my tears, Anna, your father didn't make it.

It wasn't the look she gave me then, but the one after that, that I'll never forget. This first one, her reaction to the information I had just given her, was blank; it conveyed nothing. She was like that for a few moments, and then she turned her head to the other side, as if she'd had enough bad news and couldn't take any more. I touched her softly as I whispered her name. And that was when she lashed out, when she turned suddenly, as suddenly as she could with that arm and that leg, and that was when she spat venom at me, get out of here, you evil bitch, I don't ever want to see you again. And that was also when she gave me that look weighed down with all the hatred in the world. I'll never forget that look, which has evolved into this one here, a look somewhere between hostile and mocking that stays with you forever.

I got up and staggered out of the room. I felt as if I had been shot in the heart, in the lungs, I couldn't breathe, I could barely take in air.

I tried to go back the next day, but they told me that her doctor had banned visitors. It was clear that she really didn't ever want to see me again. It was over and I had to get past it somehow.

I had to forget Anna's conclusive and final goodbye that was so tragic and hurtful, but I also had to forget Maties. At first it was terrible, I saw him everywhere, around every corner. I imagined I saw him on the street, even though I knew full well he was dead because I was the one who had organized his funeral because, with Anna still in the ICU, there was no one else to do it. Accepting the loss of someone's constant presence in your life is a dreadfully grueling test, Maties had been always by my side and when he wasn't we spoke on the phone, checking in with each other about our concerns and problems. We had been together for a year and, if it weren't for Anna, we surely would have been living together soon. And every time I saw Maties in my head, I saw Anna next to him, looking at me with that hateful gaze and saying, get out of here, you evil bitch. For the first few days, that hurt me more than losing Maties. Anna had known exactly where and how hard to throw her poison dart to wound me deeply, and forever.

So forgetting it all was a long, very difficult process. To tell the truth, I haven't forgotten any of it, but at least after the first year I began to be able to look toward the future and think that I had to find my own way to go on. Before that, I hadn't been able to walk without dragging that festering wound with me, reopening with each step, causing me excruciating pain. The image of Maties blended with the image of Anna. I told myself that one day, after much time had passed, I would talk to her again, because I couldn't stand to think that it had all ended like that. Sometimes, in the middle of class, I would leave my student alone, saying I had to go to the bathroom, and I would go cry because I couldn't take it anymore. The student would look at me afterwards with an expression of pity that spoke volumes; it was obvious that I had gone to break down in tears.

Later, I decided to let go of the problem with Anna. There was nothing I could do about it; it was a waste of my time and I had to accept that. And I think I did accept it. The wounds were starting to heal. It would still be a long time before I felt entirely better, but I learned to look ahead, to see what was around me and listen to the birds, smell the flowers, and make real music again. Some colleagues at the conservatory asked me to be part of a quartet, and I agreed. We started to perform concerts around Catalonia and then some farther afield. We did that for a few years, we had a good time, and that worked as a medicine on my pain. Between that and the teaching, I was back to my old self. I didn't see Anna again, I suppose she was avoiding me, requesting a class in a time slot when she knew I wouldn't be around. And she must have been almost done with her studies anyway; that is if she continued them after the accident.

And a few years later, Karl called me. He left a message at the conservatory saying he wanted to talk. I called him back and, in his German-inflected Catalan, he explained that he had heard me in a couple of concerts and really liked my playing. That, if I was interested, we could do a test with several pieces he had to perform in a series of concerts. It wasn't the tour of Bach's double concerto yet— but, of course, I said that I would be thrilled to audition. I mentioned it to the other members of the quartet. Watch out, the cellist said with a smile, that guy stops at nothing. What do you mean, he stops at nothing? I asked. Just that; that he's broken the heart of every musician who's played with him. Come on, that must be an exaggeration, I said. Suit yourself, she replied mysteriously.

After her comments, my curiosity was piqued. But that was the least of it. I was so proud that Karl T. had called me; he was a German who asked for political asylum in the time of the Iron Curtain and became the voice of musical truth in this country. I had originally been wary of the whole operation. The truth is, I don't trust those kind of categorizations, and when someone is so renowned I always think that there must be personal and political interests behind their reputation. But I bit my tongue when I heard his orchestra, which he had created here with people I knew, who played the best they could in dreadful groups—but he was able to bring them together and channel them in such a way that baroque music,

Bach in particular, began to sound like I'd imagined it sounded in its own time. I left that concert convinced that, from that moment on, I would consider the name Karl T. a guarantee of quality. And that was why, when he called, I came running.

We did a series of concerts around the country, coming and going; Karl didn't like to spend too many days on the road. But first we did the audition, that test of my soul. You have to use your fingers more and your soul a bit less, he said, so I would understand. And then I played differently, in a way that seemed rigid to me: more like Anna would have played. And then he was pleased, you're hired, he said with a smile, and for me it was as if it had suddenly started to rain in the middle of a summer drought. And I thought about the dump, the Stainer, Maties, Anna, and I said to myself that, with what was happening to me now, I was finally over it.

Karl wasn't much of a talker, but he did demand a lot of rehearsals. We will do them here, at first, you and I, and then we'll join the orchestra. And when he said here, he meant at his house, in a house where we were alone except for a maid named Maria, and his German son, Mark, who was never there because he was always studying or playing abroad, according to what I heard from my colleagues at the conservatory, who knew everything.

We began to rehearse. Karl was tough, he wanted everything perfect, we would go over it again and again, one more time, he'd say when I thought that I'd finally gotten it right, but he had a way of interpreting the music that he wanted me to capture exactly. And we worked for many, many hours, and we started to understand each other. Karl had a gaze that went deep into my brain. I began to think that I understood perfectly what he wanted, and that he and I understood each other wonderfully; I started to feel drawn in by his gaze, it was Music with a capital *M,* what I had been searching for, what I wanted most, and which Mark, with all due respect, has never been able to reach.

I would have done anything with Karl. He had wiped Maties from my memory, along with Anna's cutting words. All that was left was him and the music. Until one day there was something more because, before I began to play, he got up and asked if he could address me informally. Of course, I said. And then he approached me, closer and closer, and it was as if I were hypnotized and couldn't move. First, he kissed me gently and then ardently, and I returned his kiss with ardor. We ended up on the sofa, like a couple of teenagers without a bed in which to make love.

Maria

When I heard Miss Teresa play, I thought that she deserved a Stainer like the one I had thrown out, that she would have done wonders with it, because that lady had real soul. But when things ended up on the sofa, Mr. Karl wouldn't call me in to listen, he didn't seem to need an audience for that.

One day when Mr. Mark was at home, it must have been Christmas or some other holiday because otherwise he was never around, he came to the kitchen to see me when his father was out, because he was looking for someone to talk to. I didn't understand him very well, honestly; he spoke a strange Spanish that he seemed to have learned at school, and his Catalan was non-existent. And he mixed in German words, the way Mr. Karl did in the beginning. Well, Mr. Mark sat down and told me all about his life. I didn't ask him to, but he wanted to chat and he said, oh, Maria, if you knew what it was like there and how things have changed, I go back often and I can hardly believe it. And he said, imagine, they could kill you for going from one side of the city to the other. And my eyes grew wide as saucers and I didn't ask why, because I already knew that one side would kill the other side, but Mr. Mark told me a string of horrible stories that seemed to go on forever, about neighbors, friends, acquaintances, who had tried to get across that wall because, just imagine, it was like a wall of a house in construction, but on one side there was nothing, they had demolished everything; it was barren land, or boarded-up windows so no one could escape, and those on the other side would look to see what was happening on our side, through their own windows, and you would see them there in the distance, and they symbolized freedom, you know. He looked at me and, as if he suddenly realized who he was talking to, said, forgive me, you don't know what I'm going on about, do you? Oh, don't worry, Mr. Mark. All right, Miss Maria, he said with a smile. And then I would realize, oh, sorry, I meant to say Mark.

Mr. Mark sat in one of the four chairs around the little kitchen table and put his feet up on another. I only met my father now because my parents separated before I had even been born, and my mother didn't want to tell him that I existed; she never told him, she only left that letter. He was referring to the letter that he had brought Mr. Karl from his ex-wife when he showed up in Barcelona. I don't know if she didn't want help, Mr. Mark said, or if she was afraid that he would try to see me and then it would have been worse, you know, because those in power thought that my father had no family in East Germany and so, when he fled, they couldn't take reprisals on anyone. Mr. Mark was yawning; it was late and we were both tired, and I was thinking that he should head off to bed and leave me to my things, and it seems he had read my mind and was getting up as he continued: My mother always criticized him, she said that he was a skirt chaser, she never understood him. When he said that, Mr. Mark looked at me and I suddenly blushed without really knowing why. Luckily, he didn't notice, and before leaving he concluded, you see, Maria, you know him better than my mother did; my father is celibate, he's like some kind of musical monk. I couldn't help adding, your father goes to the depths of music. He turned from the doorway: exactly, that's what I meant, good night.

I stood there with my mouth hanging open, watching him head off to bed, I couldn't believe he could be so blind, and I told myself that sometimes it seems we know everything about somebody and, really, we know nothing, or very little. And Mr. Mark knew nothing about his father just like he hasn't a clue about his wife, Mrs. Anna. And maybe it's better that way, maybe it's better to float on a sea of innocence, there are fewer problems.

They just played the last note of the Bach concerto, pulling me from my thoughts. Mr. Mark gives some instructions. Mrs. Anna listens, as does Miss Teresa. Then they each go their own way without even looking at each other. Mr. Mark turns and searches for me with his eyes.

"Let's go, Maria," he orders.

Let's go, let's go. I get up heavily, my legs hurt and my stomach is churning. Miss Teresa notices and comes over to help me.

"Come on, Maria, we're done. Tomorrow is the real concert. You have to wear that lovely dress you showed me—"

I laugh a little. She and Mr. Mark treat me like a little girl. Anna treats me like a leper.

Mr. Karl treated Miss Teresa with kid gloves, honestly. He

would lay her on the sofa and caress her everywhere, and she looked like she was in ecstasy; she wasn't like the other women, not like that first opera singer who just laughed and yelped like a madwoman. Teresa was very young, maybe fifteen years younger than Mr. Karl, but it was obvious she was enthralled with her conductor and I felt very bad thinking that it would end, because it always did. I was very shocked, because on the first day they rehearsed at home, he told her she had too much soul. And that was more or less just what he had told me.

One day he'd told me that not only do people have souls, but that violins do, too. And he had me look through the long hole in the instrument's box, the sound box, as he called it. Do you see that little stick? he asked. Yes, I see it, I answered. I saw a little stick that went from the bottom to the top, beneath the bridge that held the strings. Well, that is the violin's soul. I looked at him thinking he was pulling my leg, but he was very serious, so I realized he wasn't. Ah, was all I said, like an idiot. And that image, of the soul in the shape of a little stick, stayed with me. Who would have thought that a soul could be like that, even if it's just an instrument's. If the priest from my town found that out . . .

We practiced German songs. There was one that I was really taken with. There were lyrics on the score but, of course, I didn't understand a word. What does it say? I asked Mr. Karl one day. Well, it talks about a shepherd's love for a peasant girl, and that his flock is white like the peasant girl's skin; that's what it says. And I thanked him, and then I played it knowing what it meant and, oh, that made it so much easier to make music, because you knew who you were talking to and what you were talking about. And I closed my eyes and played it like never before, and that was one that Mr. Karl had made me go over many times, always correcting me. And when I finished, I opened my eyes and was surprised to find that he had been crying. Very good, Maria, thank you, he said. And I already knew that when he wanted me to leave he would always say thank you. I placed the violin down gently on a chair and I left, passing as quietly as I could past Beethoven on my way to the kitchen and my bedroom. And I wondered why he had cried, maybe because he hadn't managed to teach me what he wanted to, even after so many years. But it didn't matter, I found it moving and that was what counted.

We didn't have class for a long time after that. I missed playing the violin and, when he wasn't there, I would pick it up and practice a little. Sometimes I played the German songs, and sometimes I tried to interpret the notes that Mr. Karl had written on some score that he'd left by the piano, or somewhere else, because we never lacked for scores around that house; I could have my pick. Among them were some real tests of skill, frantic races to play note after note and maintain a speed throughout, that I was incapable of doing. Secretly I tried it; I spent a whole week when Mr. Karl was traveling, but I couldn't do it. And, when I realized that I never would be able to, I began to cry. I cried softly for a long time. It was obvious that I could put soul and feelings and whatever else into it but that I'd never be really fast, it was impossible—for that I'd have to spend a whole lifetime doing exercises like the ones that Mr. Karl and Miss Teresa and all the violinists who came over to the house had done. Obviously, Mr. Karl told me one day that he no longer went fast because he no longer played the violin, and he wouldn't be able to do a *presto*, he said it like that, just the way it sounds, *presto*, and I didn't know what a *presto* was, but I nodded because it sounded like pressured, and later, I found out that it was a piece of music played very fast, so I thought, *Look at that, I was right. Brava, Maria*, I said to myself.

This plush hall is nothing like my little apartment, and nothing like the house where I lived for so many years. It's not even anything like the room where I used to play for Mr. Karl and where, with his help, I managed to make music—or at least that was the feeling I had. This lovely hall is completely different, made for sensitive ladies and gentlemen to come and hear music. And tomorrow I will come to hear music here, and they told me that they'd save me a seat in the middle of the third row because the first row is too close and you can't see a thing.

With Miss Teresa, reaching the depths of music lasted longer than with the others. Mr. Karl came to see me one day in the kitchen, I knew that he wanted to have a hot chocolate, and I made it for him. He never had his hot chocolate in the dining room, just as he had never taken a woman to his bed. The dining room was for lunch and dinner, and his bed only for sleep. Extra things took place on the sofa and in the kitchen. That day he talked again about music and women. I hope that you understand it some day, he said, coughing a little and looking at me out of the corner of his eye to see what effect his words had on me. I didn't say a word, just kept working, I didn't know if he was asking me whether I understood it already or whether he was saying that eventually I would. In fact, I was so used to his behavior that I never thought about understanding it or not, like we don't try to understand breathing, we just breathe. And it was the same with Mr. Karl, just a part of him and I wondered if all musicians were like that, if they all wanted to reach the depths of music—until I met Mr. Mark and I realized that no, not all musicians did that, it was just Mr. Karl. And another thing that I was starting to grasp was that I didn't make real music because he never wanted anything with me, and if I played like those violinists who came to the house, I imagine he would have tried something with me too. At night, when I closed my eyes, I tried to imagine myself on that sofa with Mr. Karl doing those things that he now did with Miss Teresa but had done with so many before her—and, like that first day when I couldn't pull my eye away from the keyhole, just like that first day, my thoughts would be transfixed by a scene in which I played the starring role. I imagined Mr. Karl kissing me, caressing me, taking off my clothes, having me put down the violin, a violin that didn't belong to me, and having me stretch out there on that black leather sofa, to mine the depths of music. And I wasn't the least bit ashamed; I went with it, and I was so mesmerized by that idea that I could feel a fire rising inside me, a fire that burned my thoughts and my soul and even my body, and those flames burned so brightly that when I opened my eyes I discovered that I really would have liked that to happen, I would have liked it a lot. But that would never come to pass, I was a maid and he was my employer. And there are things that can never be forgotten, even with a violin in the mix.

Do you think she plays well? he asked me that day in the kitchen, to change the subject. I knew he was talking about Miss Teresa, but I pretended I didn't: Who do you mean, sir? Her, he clarified, and there I couldn't get out of it because we both knew full well who "her" was in that moment, the woman who had been spending a lot of time on the sofa in the past few months, longer than the others had lasted, surely because they were preparing more concerts together, not just one, and so that extended their relationship. Mr. Karl, his mouth filled with hot chocolate and whipped cream, was waiting for my response, and I left him waiting, because I always thought, *What if I stick my foot in it?* because, obviously, he just kept asking me what I thought about how this one or the other one played, but I could make a mistake. I didn't dare to say anything about Miss Teresa at first: I don't understand, sir, I'm not one of you, I'm no musician, you should ask someone like—I ended my sentence there because he cut me off, banging his spoon against his cup and almost choking as he rushed to tell me, Maria, don't say that, you have an excellent ear and it's a shame you weren't born into a musical family. Then I piped up, with dignity, and said, pardon me, sir, but I *was* born into a musical family. He gave a start: Really? Yes, I answered, my parents were *cantaores* in Andalusia. Since he was shocked speechless, I explained: They played and sang the popular music of the South, flamenco music, and my mother danced, too, and they wanted me to dance and sing, but I left there when I was very young and I only ended up singing at my First Communion.

I could see that Mr. Karl was very surprised, and you didn't learn to read music? he asked. No, sir, I said, it was all by ear, we do it differently down there. I didn't know what else to tell him, and I wasn't sure why I had got into all that. Then he said, as if talking to himself, oh, now I understand why you sang at the beginning. I felt vindictive and, in an offended tone, I said, yes, but you didn't like it, sir, and I stopped. He had already finished his hot chocolate, and I took away the cup and saucer to wash it. I was waiting for him to leave but he didn't, oh, Maria, now I feel bad after hearing that, he said in the end, but it was impossible for me to play or compose with you singing like that.

I didn't try to figure out what he meant by singing like that, I just let it go. Instead, I put down the rag for a moment to look at him and say, Mr. Karl, you taught me to make real music, and I'll never be able to thank you enough. I didn't know how else to tell him that I was deeply grateful, that was just how it came out. He muttered something and left. I remember that the days were short, that Christmas was approaching, because there were lights and joy on the streets, but it was already quite dark and it wasn't that late. I remember that, just as I was heading to my room, he rang the bell from the piano room, and I thought, *What does he want now?* I was tired, that day, I don't remember why, but I wanted to turn in for the night.

He was waiting for me beside the piano. First, he said, forgive me, but you didn't tell me what you think of her playing. He didn't say Teresa, just her, all the time. I'll get straight to the point, sir, she's the best you've ever had. Mr. Karl was still for a moment, then he nodded slightly. Then, without saying a thing, he handed me the violin. It's already tuned, he said. Please, play the song about the shepherd and the peasant girl. He had a strange expression and asked me as if it were a matter of life and death. I didn't dare reply and I picked up the violin, that student instrument that, in spite of everything, I knew had a soul and produced such sad sounds that they inevitably hurt when you tried to reproduce them. I got ready to play, and then he said, one second, and he began an introduction on the piano. I don't know where it came from but I had never heard it before. At one point he lifted his chin to mark my entrance, just the way he did with all those other women; he wanted me to play with him the way they did, and he offered to accompany me like he did for them. I began and the first slide of the bow came out shaky, but that was it. It was like heaven with the piano. The room, the house, all of it, had ceased to exist; it was only me and Mr. Karl and the music, and the story of the love between a shepherd and a peasant girl that, according to what he'd told me, didn't end well. The sounds that I myself was making transported me to another world. I understood why they say that music calms the savage beast, I understood why they say that music has healing powers, I understood why they say all those things about music. I understood it that day, all of a sudden, playing a German song about a peasant girl and a shepherd with Mr. Karl.

When the song was over, I opened my eyes and he got up all of a sudden, in quite a state, as if he were having trouble breathing, as if he'd been very moved by the music. He came over to me and I stayed stock-still and I thought, *Holy Virgin of the Macarena, we're about to end up on the sofa.* Mr. Karl stopped in front of me. At first he didn't do anything, he was just a few inches from my face, rocking back and forth as if he were dizzy. Then, it seemed that he made up his mind, and he looked at me for a few seconds with an expression I'll never forget, and all he said was, take off your uniform please. I didn't make him ask twice and I put my hands behind my back to untie my apron. He gave me a last look, one of those that fuse with your soul forever, and then he left. He went out of the room and, shortly afterwards, I heard the door to the street open and close behind him.

The

Concert

Mark

The hall is filled with people. When I made my entrance, the orchestra stood up and everyone applauded. I turn and look at the audience and am completely blinded because all the spotlights are on me. I have butterflies in my stomach, I always do before a concert, the adrenaline pumps up and down and ends up settling where it needs to settle to create that mix of excitement and fear. Later, we replace that fear with satisfaction; that must be what we are all looking for when we break out of our usual routine, when we do things that make us nervous, that shake us up, and that we do despite all that. That must be it.

I didn't think to ask if there was a microphone. I clear my throat and start to speak loudly, projecting so that everyone can hear me. Soon there is absolute silence.

"Good evening. As you all know, my father died ten years ago, on his way to Vienna, after conducting a concert identical to the one we will perform tonight, here in Berlin. My father was from East Germany, but he fled and settled in Barcelona. He was already a well-known conductor and the Catalans offered him political asylum, a home, and the working conditions he needed. But he always wanted to come back here, and he was able to with a concert at the Staatsoper, where he had played and conducted in more difficult times. Now the theater is temporarily closed, which is why we are here, at the Schiller—"

I took in a large breath before continuing:

"This concert, as you've seen on the program, is a selection of baroque music that includes some of Monteverdi's *canzonettas,* some arias by Purcell and Handel, and a few short pieces by different composers in the first part. The second is devoted entirely to Bach, and it ends with the *Concerto for Two Violins,* a piece that meant so much to my father, and which we have chosen to play here with the same violinists he chose for the Berlin concert ten years ago. Thank you so much for your support."

They applaud again and then there is silence, that silence before the start of a concert, that holding your breath before launching an attack, a musical attack. I had been wondering if I should talk to the audience about myself and my experiences in East Berlin, but in the end I decided not to. It's also exciting for me to come here, even though the renovations mean we are in the West at the Schiller instead of in the East at the Staatsoper, the Staatsoper where I had attended so many concerts and where I had also played the cello with the orchestra. But if I explain that, they won't understand why my father was in Barcelona and I wasn't, and then it all gets too complicated, and I don't want to make him look bad; after all, he didn't even know I existed.

I hope he didn't know, that is; there are always doubts about what really happened, if he knew that my mother was pregnant and whether or not they told me the truth. I hope they did, and I believed my father's shocked face as he read the letter I brought to him in Barcelona from my mother, when he looked at me suspiciously as if he wasn't sure that I was really his son.

But Mark, how can you worry about such things now? There's no point. We always have our doubts, always. I also doubt Anna sometimes; I know that there are things she hasn't told me and never will. I only know that she never lets me leave her side; it's as if she needs me constantly, and that sometimes feels like it's suffocating me— because I don't know how to live like that, I need my space and I need to work alone, I'm a musician. At first I thought that it would pass, but later, I realized it wouldn't, it wouldn't pass, because it was going on for too long. And now she's been grumbling because she wants to have a child, and I can't really imagine it. I don't have time to take care of a child and I don't think she does either, because she spends all her time with her Stainer. It's when she's practicing that I can slip away, because otherwise it's impossible. And, since she needs to rehearse for hours, I get the time I need. It's also good when she is working for someone else; they hire her more and more because they say she's the violinist with the most agile fingers in all of Europe. And I'm not sure she really is, but she is definitely agile and can play fast passages at supersonic speed. If the baroque composers could see her, they'd be amazed. I don't think there was anyone in that period who could play so fast. Now we do everything in a rush, rushing to try to get everything done in time, with the clock ticking, and Anna is that way too, sometimes only just managing to prepare in time for her concerts and tours.

How could we take care of a child under these conditions? It's impossible. And it doesn't make sense to have kids just to leave them with a governess; I think children should be with their parents. Besides, I suspect she only wants to have a kid to keep me with her. And since she's getting older, she must be worried that she's running out of time. And she really is running out of time, and she really should get on that. But not with me, no way, not with me.

Anna

This morning I took a pregnancy test and it came back positive. So I'm more nervous than ever about this concert. Mark and I are going to be parents. I know that he doesn't want to have kids, but I don't care. And when I go back to Barcelona, I'll go to the doctor so he can tell me what I need to do, because at my age you have to be extra careful with a pregnancy. Today, I feel like jumping for joy; today, everything is different, because I know that I'm going to have a child, and that Mark won't be able to leave my side.

I always get nervous when I'm waiting to start playing, it's true, but today is different: I'm even more nervous because I have to play Bach's double concerto, Karl's favorite piece. He knew it so well it was almost as if he'd composed it himself. I've stayed in the dressing room to avoid waiting at the stage door with Teresa; I already have to be next to her through the whole concert. Look, that way we'll both be more calm. That way I can also practice my part of the piece, even though she's the one who should be practicing, and instead she's just standing there, calm as can be, beside the stage.

How old must she be now? Something like sixty I'd guess, because she was already a lot older than me when I was her student. She won't be playing for much longer, no, she won't be able to. And she can't keep up with me; she's not fast enough. But Mark refused to listen to me and he had her come for this. He said that his father would have wanted it that way, and that there must be a reason for that. Honestly, I think she and I are like apples and oranges in every way, including musically. Teresa and I are absolutely nothing alike.

The little baby inside me must be starting to move even though it's a tiny little thing, like a pea or maybe even smaller, I don't know because I don't know about those things, but my little guy is in there and someday it'll be a child and maybe play the violin or maybe the cello like its father, or maybe the piano, or maybe it'll be an opera singer. Or maybe it won't be a musician, I don't know, but it will be my child and will stay with me all my life, and Mark will stay with us too; he'll stay with me and we'll parent together and have a family like no other in the world. A family like the one I never had, that has nothing to do with my mother, or my father, or Teresa.

That evil witch didn't even come to see me when I got out of the hospital. I asked the doctor not to allow any visitors. I did that so she would want to see me even more, so she would need me, and so, when I got out of the hospital, she would be there for me. And none of that came to pass. I had no one, I needed her and she didn't come. I hated her then as much as I do now. She forgot about me, she abandoned me, she left me to my fate, like everybody else. She totally deserves that I keep her Stainer and parade it around in front of her.

She also totally deserves to have lost her Maties. But I don't. When she told me that Papa had died, I thought my world was ending. What point was there to him dying and not me? I had done that so that we would both die at the same time, so we would leave this world united forever. And so she would find out that we had an accident and we were both dead and that she was left alone. And so Mama would find out some day too, even though at that point I didn't know if she was alive or dead. I only knew that on that day so many years ago, she had left all of a sudden, off to some paradise where there were no little girls who wiped snot on her dresses, and where there were surely men waiting to take her out, where she had someone like Clara on hand to hear her announce, around seven in the evening: Today, I won't be home for dinner.

And my suffering would be over. I would have left a world that wasn't prepared for a girl like me; that would have been the end of my broken heart over losing my mother and then my father. Because, when I'd finally managed to get to know him, I'd lost him to an opportunist who, pretending to be my friend, stole the only life I had from me. An opportunist who, if she had really been my friend, would have come to see me when I got out of the hospital and ended up home alone with the maids, who stayed with me day and night after I agreed to pay them the overtime, because oh, lord, all of a sudden I was the one in charge of all of Papa's money, which frankly was quite a lot, and, being bedridden, I was able to do little with. And I cried thinking of him and I told myself that I had to also look after financial matters, and all of it at the same time was too much for me.

I was alone for many days, alone with those three women, two during the day and one at night. I was in my bedroom looking out the window, and I saw the lake with its stagnant water, the one that had captured my soul and would hold it forever.

Yesterday, after rehearsal, I got Mark to come with me to stroll by the Spree. It was dark, everything was damp and black. But with just a glance, I clearly spotted my imprisoned soul. What are you smiling about? Mark asked me, looking at me intrigued and trying to head the other way. Oh, nothing, I answered, holding him there tightly; the water makes me smile, you know I like water. I always tell everyone that I like water, because otherwise they can't understand why I stop every time I see it. And not only do I like water, but rivers make a well-enunciated music that gets into your ears and some part of your brain, where memories of the dead and the living who have moved on are stored.

I'm done with my practicing. I put the Stainer to one side and sit down in the armchair in this dressing room. At intermission I will head toward the stage and wait for the moment to play the Bach concerto—the moment to do what I love most in the world, which is to show off my agility in front of Teresa, who's already on her last legs as a violinist, but also as a human being. Because time passes for everyone including her; there's no way around it, no matter how much make-up she wears. A few more years and I won't have to worry about seeing her around because she won't be able to play any notes, not the fast ones and not the slow ones. *Just have a little more patience, Anna.*

Maria

Today of all days, I would have stayed under the covers, I don't even know how I sit through an entire concert anymore; this is really getting to be too much, when I get back to Barcelona I'll have to see the doctor. But I can't lose my courage now, not now when I have work to do, because I have to follow through on what I came here to do.

Miss Anna showed up at the house six months before Mr. Karl died. Oh, it wasn't that he had ended things with Miss Teresa, no, not by a long shot, instead they both spent time on the sofa, at least until they were both practicing together. Before Miss Anna, the whole time he was with Teresa there was no one else, and I'm talking about at least two or three years. I thought that Mr. Karl was getting on in years, and that when he'd asked me to take off my uniform it had somehow been a turning point in the way he looked at things.

I had taken off my uniform, just as he asked, and I put it away in the closet. Then came the difficult task of having to buy clothes, because, obviously, if I didn't wear a uniform around the house, I had to wear something, and all I had were things I wore on Thursdays and Sunday mornings, I had never had the need for anything more. When I took off my uniform, I realized that I was getting older. I tried to put on the dress I used to wear when I went out with that boyfriend who wanted me to let him touch me, and it didn't fit anymore. I looked in the mirror and, suddenly, I discovered a face run through with sunken lines that had become wrinkles, some big ones and a lot of small ones. And I looked at my hair and saw it was gray. I no longer wore that ponytail from when I went out with that man after mass, but I did always pull my hair back into a bun so it wouldn't be in my face. All of a sudden, I wondered if I should have let him touch my inner thigh, and maybe I would have had a husband and kids, and maybe I would have lived in a different house—smaller but just for me, like the apartment I have now, or on the other side of the city, who knows? But I definitely wouldn't have learned to play the violin, and I definitely wouldn't have had Mr. Karl for a teacher. I'm sure I wouldn't have felt the way I felt in Mr. Karl's house, doing whatever I pleased and setting everything up the way I wanted to, as if it were my very own house. And I definitely wouldn't have had a Beethoven to dust and say *gut'n Tag* to.

I like it better this way, without a uniform; what do you think? he'd asked me when he saw that I'd taken it off. I looked at myself a little, I didn't know what to say, I don't pay attention to these things, but I guess I agree. Come on, play, he said then, and he closed his eyes.

I was surprised that he asked me to play when Miss Teresa was still on active duty; I mean, while Miss Teresa was still spending time on the sofa at every rehearsal. Normally, when there were women on active duty, he would forget about teaching me. But after that thing about the uniform and after Miss Teresa, everything was different, and Mr. Karl kept up his classes with me. So I kept playing and studying with him, and he no longer cried, but he was distant and so serious that I sometimes thought he was mad at me. And I would play and play, all those German songs that tore at the heart of whoever heard them. Mr. Karl had given me a record so I could hear how they were sung. And now you have to do the same with the violin, he told me. And I was about to reply, sir, but the violin can't sing, but I bit my tongue because I suddenly realized that it wasn't true, that the violin can sing, of course it can, and it could sound even more melancholy than if you added lyrics, and that was what Mr. Karl was talking about.

When he wasn't there, I played even more. I would play as much as I could, more and more each day. I let myself be carried off by those songs that spoke of distant lands but with a sadness that was universal, the same sadness that women and men feel all over the world. Sometimes I had to rush afterwards to finish all my daily chores in the house, because I would get carried away by my playing; I couldn't stop. I knew all those songs by heart. Mr. Karl congratulated me every time he heard me playing them, and he told me that he would have to bring me another score because I already knew that one very well. He would smile and say thank you, in that distant tone he often had then, and I would leave but not before nodding my head slightly, like the start of a bow, which I always did, since the first day I had shown up at that house, something my mother had taught me I had to do with gentlemen who had more money than us. And, from that first day, I had figured that Mr. Karl had quite a bit more money than I did.

Everything I'm hearing is lovely; it's music that reaches the depths of your heart, and the singers aren't like that first one I heard on the sofa. No, they're much more discreet, and they sound more like they're talking than screeching to break glass. It's almost as if they're playing the violin. And it is really a switch, as if the violin were the human voice.

Mrs. Anna, who also plays the violin, showed up at the house like the next big thing. Today, one of the country's top violinists will be coming, Mr. Karl told me early one morning, prick up your ears and have a listen, Maria. Yes, sir, I said obediently. I already knew that Mr. Karl was going to tour Europe with the orchestra, one singer and two violinists to perform the Sunday-morning Bach concerto. One of those violinists was Miss Teresa, and I was pleased about that, because, even though she would spend time on the sofa with Mr. Karl, she's obviously a good person, always smiling and kind with me—not like some of the others who acted like they couldn't even see me, and would go straight to the piano room without my permission, when I was the one who was supposed to allow them in or not, according to what Mr. Karl had told me to tell them.

Miss Anna was one of those. And, when she finished the first, strictly musical, session with Mr. Karl, he came to find me in the kitchen and asked me what I had thought of her playing. I didn't know what to tell him, because early that morning he himself had told me that she was the best violinist in the country, and I didn't get that impression at all, but in the end I screwed up my courage and said, she plays notes. He lowered his head, yes, you're right, she plays notes, very, very fast, but nothing more; this one has no soul, she's the opposite of Teresa, and I have to put them together to do this tour; I think I've made a mistake with this girl. That day he didn't have any hot chocolate, just a glass of water, and he left again. I need to think, he murmured, and I could see that he wasn't in a very good mood. When he passed by Beethoven, instead of saying *gut'n Tag,* that day he gave him a slap, as if he was blaming the plaster musician for all the world's evils.

Mr. Karl ended up taking both of them on tour. I think he decided to try to find a common meeting point, somehow bring them together. That was what I deduced after listening to him instruct them. He had only given Miss Anna one audition, but he gave her another chance. He told her to put a little more of herself into it, and then I remember that she did and that Mr. Karl was satisfied with that. Now I think that she didn't really put more of herself into it, she just pretended to; she knew how to fake, musically speaking, a sensitivity she didn't have. And that faking is what got her where she is now, and also into the arms of Mr. Mark who seems like he can't live without her.

Miss Anna spent time on the sofa when it seemed like she was the violinist that he needed. It was the day she brought in the Stainer. I also thought she played very well that day, even though I didn't like her at all, not only because she ignored me when she walked through the door but also because of the attitude she always had, whether she was walking or sitting still or playing the violin. She was tall and thin, with very dark hair and skin, she seemed more from my region than from Catalonia, and she walked confidently on stiletto heels that would have surely made me fall over. There was silence when Mr. Karl said, okay, you're hired, and then I put my eye to the keyhole and I saw what I was expecting to see. Another woman on active duty, I remember thinking, and this time it didn't seem that Teresa had been dismissed yet. Nor did it seem he had any intention of dismissing her, Mr. Karl was doing a concerto for two violins, and so those two violinists, both of them, had to be protagonists in his life. That was new; it had never happened before and I wasn't sure how Mr. Karl would pull it off. *I hope they never run into each other,* I thought.

Of course, they did run into each other. And I'll never forget that day. It seems that Mr. Karl hadn't told either of them that the other one would be there, and they found out for the first time right then, one day when they came to rehearse together. And, Holy Virgin of the Macarena, it seemed they knew each other and didn't like each other very much. I still remember when I opened the door to the piano room so Miss Anna could go in, and Miss Teresa was already inside. I couldn't see Miss Anna's face, but I could see Miss Teresa's, and it was a mix of shock, incredulousness, and exasperation. She didn't smile. I remember that Mr. Karl said, this is her, and I remember Miss Anna announcing, we've already met. They didn't even shake hands, and Miss Teresa said, wow, it's been years. Then, Mr. Karl, who thought on his feet and saw that something was going on, started to talk about music, and all three started to play. And that they did well together, and I was shocked to see how Mr. Karl truly managed to bring them together, to unite those two different ways of making music, one that flowed from the soul and the other based in agility and technique.

But about a month before that, just days before that strange, curious encounter, the thing with the Stainer happened. Miss Anna came to the house with the Stainer. I'm sure she wanted to impress Mr. Karl, and she did, but not the way she was imagining. He asked her for the violin for a moment and came to see me with the instrument in his hand. And I, who was pretending to dust Beethoven, almost fell to the floor trying to get away quickly. Maria, he called to me when he found me in the entryway. Either he hadn't realized I'd been behind the door or he didn't care; all he cared about was the violin. He looked at me with his eyes gleaming, is it ours, he questioned me in a whisper, and he put one of the instrument's long holes up to my face so I could read some letters inside that said something about Stainer, and that was when a little light went on inside my head after all those years and I understood why he called the violin Stainer. And look at this, Mr. Karl suddenly pointed. And I looked and it was the mark of a crack on one corner that someone had repaired. I understood; maybe when it fell from the cart or at the dump, I suggested, blushing, but I don't know, it's been so many years. Yes, he said, looking at it, and then he repeated, it's been so many years.

He had said ours, and I found that unsettling. Despite that, I looked at it as professionally as I could. The truth is that I had never really looked at it when it was in the house, except for that day when I threw it out. I'm not sure, sir, I answered. I am, he said, it's ours, it's the one from Salz—something or other. And before heading back to the piano room, he said: Obviously someone made a business out of that garbage.

I kept quiet so I could hear what Miss Anna said, but he didn't ask her where it had come from. Maybe he didn't want to embarrass her for having pulled a violin from the trash. Or maybe she had bought it from a junkman, even though she seemed to have money. Whatever the case, and knowing Mr. Karl, he surely must have thought that if he asked her where she had gotten the Stainer, he would have made her look bad. That's how Mr. Karl was. But she must have felt she owed him an explanation and, in a voice loud enough for me to hear, she said, oh, I've had it for many years; it was a gift from my father. He bought it here? Mr. Karl then asked. And she replied, I don't know, but he's dead now so I can't ask him. And that was the end of it. I didn't hear anything more. They spoke softly and quickly, and the telephone rang and I had to go answer it. I returned just as another sofa scene was starting. I didn't hear the violin again. What I do know is that Miss Anna eventually ended up giving him the instrument in exchange for something. I only learned later what it was. And that was how the Stainer with the crack, that incredibly valuable violin that I had thrown into the garbage by mistake, came back to the house after many years. And one day, Mr. Karl had me come to the piano room and said, play one of those songs, and he handed me the Stainer. It was an emotional moment for me; I had thrown it away before I knew it could make such sounds, and now I was able to play it.

With trembling hands I took the instrument and began to play. I already knew that when Mr. Karl said "one of those songs," he meant the ones from his country and particularly the one about the peasant girl and the shepherd. So that was the one I played. I was captivated, because it turned out that the violin made magic: It was as if it held the sun inside it or something like that. My God, I exclaimed, stopping after a few bars. Oh, keep playing, please, said Mr. Karl, exasperated, as if I had cut short the ecstatic state he seemed plunged into. Yes, I said, yes, slowly and gently. And I started playing again. I played alone, without the piano. I closed my eyes and let the Stainer do it all. And I reached the end of the piece as if I had traveled in an enchanted ship. Finally, I opened my eyes and said, sir, this is a magical violin. He said yes, without even looking at me and my heart sank a little because lately he was so odd.

It seemed like I should leave, and that was when I thought of something even stranger, which was that when Miss Anna played there was no magic. When Miss Anna played the Stainer, it sounded like a normal violin. So it was obvious that the Stainer wasn't always magic; it depended on who was playing it. I went to the kitchen, perplexed and silent as the grave, and Mr. Karl just kept staring at the piano without even saying goodnight to me.

I was able to play the Stainer from then on, but only occasionally, when he wasn't there, because he didn't allow it when he was. No, play the student violin, he would say, that's what it's for. And he gave me the other one, and I played like always, and I went through the lessons he had told me to learn. I played as best I could, but obviously I noticed a big difference between that violin and the Stainer; it was like night and day.

That was a very unusual period. Mr. Karl wasn't himself, and the Stainer was back. But I was starting to think that, despite the magic it made, maybe it would have been better if that violin had stayed wherever it had been. Because now that we had it back it was as if it had cast a spell on us, like the ones Andalusian gypsy women would cast if they didn't like you or if someone asked them to bring harm to you. Everything had changed color and we, he and I, were getting old. And it made me sad because I thought that maybe Mr. Karl had expected more of me when I played the Stainer and I'd disappointed him because, after all, I was just a maid, and maids aren't violinists, not in or out of uniform.

And that day came when Miss Anna and Miss Teresa met up, and then they began the rehearsal. And there were no sofa scenes when they were both there, and I don't know if he was thinking of having them both on the sofa at the same time, but if that was his plan, it didn't come to pass, because they obviously couldn't stand each other. And, of course, in order to do certain things with another person, you have to really be able to stand them.

So from then on, I only heard music when he was with those two women, the same ones who will play at the end of this concert, and it was always one piece of music in particular. I got used to hearing them rehearse Bach's double concerto, a live version in addition to the recordings played every Sunday morning. Miss Teresa would come in first, a sweet but decisive entrance, compelled by a force that, despite everything, that woman obviously had in her. And, shortly after, Miss Anna would make her entrance, and it seemed she was competing, even though I knew they would both reach the end of the piece at the same time. And they went on like that, with Mr. Karl interrupting them every once in a while and making them repeat certain bars and passages, all very serious, all very strict. And then, when they'd finished, they'd each head off in their own direction, and Mr. Karl would stay there staring at the piano, and I would think, there's something wrong with this man.

And that was when he said, we're leaving next week. I'll be away for fifteen days.

Teresa

I hear Anna doing scales in her dressing room. We're opposites, she and I. I leave it for the very last minute, just warm up my fingers a little bit, while she spends those last moments walking. She did the same thing when we were on tour here ten years ago, too. I don't know if she'll do it today. I take a look and it's raining, and all the leaves on the ground have turned into a skating rink. And anyway, you can't see a thing. This country is so dark . . . I don't know if the concert was a good idea, opening up old wounds that took so long to scar, at least for me. Every time I see her, that dark, painful story comes into my head, and every time I have to pull myself together and bite my tongue to keep from saying something I'll regret.

But this concert wasn't anything like that first time. Karl had been being a bit mysterious about it all, he hadn't even told me whether the other violinist was a man or a woman, all he would say was that I would like them. First, he said he didn't want to tell me because he was still choosing between a few options, but then, when he had her chosen, he still wouldn't tell me. He just said, tomorrow

I will introduce you to your rival in the double concerto. Rival or complement, depending on how you look at it, of course, and I think that the two melodies weave together and complement each other, sure, but they also play at outdoing each other until they reach the end at exactly the same time. In the case of Anna, though, our game was pure rivalry; there was no possible complementing each other. When I saw her there, when Maria escorted me to the piano room, all I could think was, my God, stop the world, I want to get off. But God didn't stop the world. It was as if the earth was sinking, as if I'd been hit head-on by a catapult. I cursed the moment when I'd neglected to say I'd only go on that tour once I knew who the second violinist would be. But until I saw Anna, I didn't care who it was; I knew that Karl would get what he needed to out of whoever it was, that he would get the best possible sound out of them, that he would make us both sound as close to the way Bach intended, as only Karl could. But I never imagined he'd choose Anna, who had, it's true, earned a reputation as a top violinist in recent years. She was somewhat in style for her ability to play the fast parts dizzyingly fast, but, I don't know, I never imagined that she was the sort of musician that Karl was looking for. And yet, she was.

She was also surprised, in fact, she seemed completely shocked. Neither of us knew what to do or say; we were alike in that at least. Karl had just mixed oil and water without realizing it, and Anna mumbled that we already knew each other, and I said something like, it's been a long time, to break the ice. Maria realized that something was wrong, because Maria, even though she hides it, is very, very clever. But Karl didn't even notice. It seemed he couldn't care less, and he said, come on, let's rehearse, and we began to rehearse and said nothing more. But playing with Anna was strange and very unpleasant, and I was very distracted that day—playing a bit mechanically and thinking that I might have to abandon the project. But, of course, I couldn't, because the tour was about to start and I would have really left Karl in the lurch.

What surprised me was that Anna didn't use the Stainer, not that day and not during the tour. I found it really odd. This tour was the obvious place to show off an instrument like that, playing in Vienna, Rome, Madrid, and Paris. But first came Berlin. Where would she play with the Stainer, if not in these European capitals? *Maybe she doesn't have it anymore,* I then thought, but she'd have to be a fool to part with it, as foolish as I had been. I also thought that there was something between her and Karl, but honestly that didn't surprise me at all. I was already counting on it, because Karl had a reputation for getting involved with any musician who worked with him and wore a skirt, even if she was much younger than him, like Anna. I had been counting on it since the very first day we got involved on that black sofa; I had always had it crystal clear and, since I had it crystal clear, I signed on to the mutual game—in which we both got our needs met. I was just happy making music with him, and I didn't demand anything more. I was content with touching heaven with my fingers thanks to his genius. What I didn't know, and would have liked to, was if Anna was aware of Karl's behavior, because Anna had always searched for people who could be hers and only hers. And Karl had never been one for monogamy.

The truth is when I went home after that first meeting with Anna at Karl's house, I thought that it's true that fate can play some dirty tricks on us, but this was truly one for the history books.

Anna

Intermission. The audience is riveted and applauding passionately. That's rare here, because this isn't Barcelona, where audience members really show their feelings. It's really strange: At first you're surprised by the different reactions between audiences from place to place when your performance is almost exactly the same. Later, you realize that the Mediterranean spectators show more feeling than the Nordics. It must be something in our blood; it runs hotter and we get emotional more easily, and we also get annoyed faster, and we have less tolerance when someone tries to pull a fast one on us. Here, on the other hand, they give a few claps and that's it, no matter how great the performance is. Well, that's what they usually do, because from what I'm hearing, tonight this concert hall is really spirited.

The rehearsals with Teresa and Karl were spirited too. Luckily, we only did two before joining the entire orchestra. And this time we just did one, right before the first orchestra rehearsal.

I pick up the violin and leave my dressing room. I see Teresa from a distance, and again I think that she's not what she used to be, I remember, not many years ago, envying her impressive physical presence. I was slim and stringy, and she was tall and strong. But now she's showing her years. And it's too late for her to have children; maybe she thought my father could have given her one, I could have had a little brother or sister. Not from that woman, ugh, what a horrible thought.

Now Mark leaves the stage, wiping the sweat from his forehead with a white handkerchief—one of those he always carries in his pocket, asking me if they're clean, and I've given the maid special instructions to prioritize Mark's handkerchiefs, to put them before even his shirts. He has an obsession with them. Now I smile at him and ask if it went well. He doesn't answer, just nods. I run to his side, to walk him to his dressing room. He doesn't pay much attention to me. He must be tired.

"Can I bring you anything?" I ask at the last minute when I see he wants to hole up in the dressing room.

"No, thanks," he says with a half-smile. "See you later, sweetie," he says, gently getting rid of me.

The door closes and I am left outside. I feel deeply wounded, run through with a blade that hit my lungs, and suddenly, I can barely breathe. It makes me think of the hospital and when I was released, because I felt that way then too. I had trouble taking in a deep breath, and the maid had to come with me everywhere because I was afraid to go alone. But that ended, and now it was happening again. It's not the first time. Sometimes Mark will do something that makes me feel like that, as if I've been hit in the lungs, hit badly. I turn around slowly and make sure no one saw the scene. I put the violin down onto a chair, carefully so that it's protected from blows, and go outside, mechanically putting one foot in front of another. There are musicians who've gone outside to smoke during the intermission, even though it's raining. Yes, it's raining, small but constant drops, the kind that fall silently and slowly soak everything, making the leaves on the ground shine. Really, it's my soul, breaking into bits and pieces; I watch it lengthen and come apart as it hits the ground and mixes in with the colorful leaves that are dark now because there's no light.

Yesterday, at the Spree, my soul flowed rapidly downstream. Not now, now it's broken into pieces.

I liked that Karl lived so close to my house, but he must not have had the lake drawn on the ceiling of his room because it wasn't as close to him as it was to me. I'm not sure; I never found out because he never showed me his bedroom. He insisted we stay in the piano room. Karl would devour me with his eyes every time we finished playing; his whole being gave off flames, and I felt myself burning, too. He was nothing like Mark, who'll never know what it's like to feel inside another person the way I felt I was inside Karl and he felt he was inside me; we were one, it was as if we didn't need anyone else in the world, and it didn't matter that he was so much older than me. I only worried about the maid showing up—but, even though she's a horrid witch, she's discreet, I'll give her that. She never walked in on us and we never heard a peep out of her.

And then there was that scene with the violin. I showed up with my Stainer to impress Karl, and he certainly was impressed—but not the way I'd hoped. He grabbed the instrument from me, looked at it carefully and asked if he could borrow it for a moment. I said yes and he left. And I thought that he must be checking something that he wanted to see alone—because there was no one else in the house, except for Maria. I still don't know what he was doing, but when he came back he was looking at me so strangely that I felt myself blushing as if he were accusing me of something. So I said the first thing that came into my head, which was that my father had given it to me, and I didn't know where he'd gotten it. And then he blurted out: How much do you want for that violin? I was shocked and, after a few seconds of silence, I answered, nothing, it's not for sale. He wasn't fazed and made me an offer. No, no, it's not for sale, I shook my head, thinking that the poor man didn't know that the only thing I had was money, that I'd lost my father and my mother, but that I was surrounded by wealth. It seemed he had let it go and we began to play. And, after we'd finished, he came over and kissed me. I had never been kissed by a man because I never let one come near me, I didn't want anyone to touch me, I didn't want anyone to profane my physical solitude, and I was already almost thirty. But I couldn't say no to him, he had me hypnotized; we were still under the effects of the outpouring of music, of that which only music can achieve—and something held me where I was, and then I felt what it was like to be kissed by a man, and not just any man but him. A man I thought was old enough to be my father, and when he died I found out that he could actually have been my grandfather. But that didn't matter in those moments: Karl kissed me passionately and, being so large and tall, it felt like he wanted to swallow me up entirely. He pushed me onto the sofa. At first I resisted a little, but he gently moved my hands away, and finally I gave in. I succumbed and I liked it, and I liked it that day and all the others that followed. I liked it until everything was ruined by the person who always ruins everything: Teresa.

But that would come later. For the moment, I had Karl just for me, even though, sometimes, he didn't remember that I was there, or he didn't pay me any attention, or we would play and then I was the one who had to go after him. And that was when I had my great idea, when I figured out how to get him to be mine and only mine. And one day I just came out and said it, I'll give you the Stainer if you marry me.

Mark

They told my father not to travel because his heart was weak. A few days before leaving for Rome he gave us a scare. Luckily, I was at home, because Maria got very flustered; she was frightened when she saw he couldn't even talk about the pain in his chest. And I leapt to the phone, an ambulance arrived, and we went to the clinic. He was back home two days later, but with very specific orders from the doctor, which he obviously ignored because they included not going on tour. The doctor told him he should drink, and that a few sips of whiskey in moments of high stress would do him good. I don't like whiskey, said my father with a scowl. The doctor got a bit angry: Well, suit yourself, I can't do anything more for you. My father zipped his lip and said no more. It seemed that the doctor had given up on him; it was as if he'd said, you can start ordering the custom coffin, because you won't fit in a regular-sized one. I wish he had because later, we really did have problems finding one that was big enough.

He had been worried for some time—but, on the outside,

he seemed the same as ever, Maria and I didn't think much of it. But when he had that angina, Maria came to me and asked, tears streaming down her face: What are we going to do, Mark, how can we keep him from going on tour? We can't, Maria, I said, shaking my head in resignation. Maria burst into tears. She was so loyal to him; that was why I insisted she had to come to this concert in Berlin, it was important that Maria come to commemorate that concert ten years ago here, on the eastern side of this city, with such a heavy past. That was the leitmotif of that whole tour: Karl T. had grown up in East Berlin, and it was very important that he return to do a concert there, once that the wall had been down for all those years. I tried to explain that to the maid, and I ended up saying: This whole tour is very important to him, but especially the concert in Berlin, and if he doesn't do it, he'll die from the disappointment. We looked at each other, and we understood each other without another word. Maria dried her tears. It was obvious that it was better he die doing what he wanted than staying home.

And that was what happened. My father did the concert in Berlin. As he was flying to Vienna alone, because the rest of the orchestra, singers, and soloists had taken another plane, he died. There was nothing anyone could do; he only suffered for the briefest second, and by the time the stewardesses realized, he was gone.

When they told me, I felt lost for many years. I mean, literally lost, because my father was my point of reference, the path I followed to reach some unknown destination in music and beyond music, since I had met him. I would have liked to have his austere lifestyle, cloak myself in that mysticism that impregnated his vocation and the rest of his life—if he had any other life, because my father lived for music.

But I'm different. I need to also live outside that world, and I need friends and I need a wife. A different wife; this one is smothering me. I think that tonight, when the concert is over, after she's finished playing, I'm going to tell her it's over. I'm fed up.

Maria heard me shout when I answered the phone, and she came running. Then she saw me crying and she heard me asking for details. With my eyes filled with tears, I moved the receiver away for a moment to tell her: He's dead. She just stood there. For a few seconds, while the orchestra manager on the other end of the line explained what had happened, she didn't move, her expression didn't change, she didn't even cry. Then she turned and vanished.

Maria

When Mr. Mark told me that his father was dead, I thought that all of a sudden the air around me had frozen. The priest had talked about the apocalypse at Mass the previous Sunday and he'd said that the heavens would fall and the earth would sink and if anyone was left alive, the angels would come down and start cutting off heads to make sure that we were all dead, because they don't call it the apocalypse for nothing. So when I heard that Mr. Karl had died, I thought that the heavens were falling and the earth was sinking. And before the angels swooped down and started cutting off heads, I went to my room, closed the door, hugged the Stainer and the letter, and I just lay there, looking at the ceiling, stretched out on the bed, for a long time. I wanted to cry and I couldn't. I had a thick, cold rock inside me that filled me up, a frozen rock that numbed me from inside. But it couldn't numb me entirely, no, because there was still a hot drop somewhere inside me and that drop gradually multiplied, and it melted the ice and made more and more drops, so many that they became a sea and all poured out.

It was hard for me to cry, but when I did I couldn't stop for hours. And, as I cried, I thought of all those years, all the things that had happened, Mr. Karl playing, Mr. Karl on the sofa, and me throwing the violin into the garbage, and making hot chocolate, and doing everything for him. And that was how I greeted the dawn, dry after many damp hours throughout the night, breaking the silence that was always there, beside that park that changed so much over the course of a day.

And it turned out that a new day had dawned, but without Mr. Karl.

After a long while, Mr. Mark came to see me. He knocked on the door and I thought that I had to open the door. I wiped away my tears and hid the Stainer in the wardrobe first. Outside there was a boy who was also crying, a boy who had lost his father. And I didn't dare to hug him, I didn't know if I should, but I wanted to, I needed it as well. He was the one who reached out to me, and we embraced, both crying, for a good long while. I don't remember having felt the warmth of another person so close in many years, I didn't remember how warm a hug could be, and Mr. Mark's hug reminded me of the ones my mother gave me when I was little, which made me feel sheltered from all the ugly things in the world.

I'm going to get everything organized, he said, after drying his tears. I'll call you for your help, okay, because we have a funeral to set up. I nodded, swallowing my tears. If he had dried away his, I had to do the same.

When Mr. Mark left, I went to the church to speak with God. God, I asked, how is it that just when you've given me everything, you take it all away? And God looked down at me from the cross he was nailed to on the other side of the altar, and he said, dear girl, complete happiness doesn't exist. Well, I don't know exactly if God said that to me, I don't remember; maybe I said it to myself, but it somehow echoed in my ears, and I started crying again, with sobs that could be heard in every corner of God's house.

I went back to the house and opened the wardrobe in my bedroom. I pulled out the Stainer and looked at it. Then, I picked up the letter that I had read so many times. I looked at it, too, but without reading it, because now that the man who had written it was dead, I couldn't find the strength—even though when he gave it to me, I read it a thousand times, at least. I saw him again, the way he had come to see me on the day he left for Berlin. He gave me such a special look when he said, come on, Maria, make me a hot chocolate with whipped cream. And I made him a hot chocolate with whipped cream. It had been a while since he'd asked me for one. I poured myself a little too and we both ate it in the kitchen, and he told me about the concert he'd prepared, and he told me he was very excited to perform that piece he always played on Sunday mornings, because he had conducted it many years ago in his country but never since then.

He wiped his lips and told me not to move. He came back a little while later, already dressed for the trip, with the Stainer in his left hand, and the bow and an envelope in his right. He looked at me in such a special way, like when I would play the song of the peasant girl and the shepherd, and he put the violin gently in my hands. I got this back for you, he told me. I couldn't believe my ears. At first I was struck dumb, but then I blurted out, Mr. Karl, you've lost your mind. But he shushed me and held out the envelope, and this is also for you. And I took the letter and was about to open it. No, he said, placing his hand on mine, open it once I've left, please. There are some things that have to be said in writing. I looked at him and, for the first time ever, I thought I saw him blushing.

The last time I saw him, he went out through the door, backlit, with his suitcase, to the waiting taxi. I would have liked to hug him, I don't know what I wanted to do to him, I had a Stainer in one hand and I couldn't believe it was mine, and I had no idea what it said in that mysterious letter, but it must have been something big because Mr. Karl wasn't the writing type. He never wrote anything except for notes on the staves. *Maybe he has written a score for me,* I thought. And I went into my room to solve the mystery that had me so intrigued, trembling with excitement, the violin in one hand and a white envelope in the other.

Teresa

The first part went quite well and there was a lot of applause. Mark left wiping his forehead and went to the dressing room followed by Anna. It seems he doesn't like her always keeping such a tight rein on him. I know why she does it; I know that Anna is, really, an unhappy soul searching for someone who will be there for her, because she had no mother and she thinks she had no father either, but that isn't true, she did have a father. Still, a normal father/ daughter relationship wasn't enough for her. She needed to have him all to herself, and, now, the only thing she has all to herself is the Stainer. So I guess I have to think of my gift as an act of charity. I don't know what to think about that girl, I just don't know what to think.

Mark insisted that I come to this concert. Ten years since Karl's death, it's an homage and they wanted everyone who played with him then to perform. He had called me up. Is Anna coming? I finally asked. Yes, he said in a thin voice. I let out a discreet uh-huh to give myself time to think. Finally I asked, and she has no problem with me coming? Mark answered immediately, oh, she wants it to be a success, like me and like everyone. *In other words,* I thought, *she doesn't want me to come.* But I knew that the idea was for the homage to be with both of us, and if I didn't go, Mark would have a real problem. And, after all, it wasn't his fault. Okay, I'll come, I agreed in the end. And on the other end of the line, I heard a relieved sigh and a thank-you that made me smile. I could put up with Anna if I had to; it wasn't like I was marrying her, it was just one concert.

The rehearsals ten years ago turned into real chess matches. Since Anna and I don't speak to each other, it was as silent as a tomb when we were together in the piano room of Karl's house. We just listened to him, we were both very attentive, and when he'd told us what he needed to, we began to play. Anna picked up her bow nervously, lines appeared on her forehead, the same ones she'd had as a child, and she played nervously as well, as if she wanted to defeat me with the notes. She really didn't have to get so worked up, I'd never be able to play as fast as her. I had other virtues, but speed wasn't one of them. I'm still not very fast, and she knows it, and she shoots me a defiant look before the start of the first and third movements, it's always the same, and I just ignore her, there's nothing to be done, and then comes the second movement, which is where I shine, because when it comes time to play with soul, Anna's lost, since she has none.

I looked at the black leather sofa and thought of days gone by, of Karl and I embracing and kissing, of Karl and I pretending we loved each other. When Karl hypnotized me for the first time, I told myself that it was a good thing and a good solution. I knew that he didn't have anyone either, that he went from woman to woman, and that there were women everywhere who were bitter after he was through with them. He paid them no mind, I think he was unable to realize the pain he caused when he moved on. Since he gave no importance to the scenes on the sofa, how was he going to imagine that his ending them abruptly could be important to anyone else?

When I sensed that Anna had also spent time on the sofa, I said to myself, Teresa, that's the end of that. My heart shrank a little, but just a little. I figured I would get over it, since I had always seen it as both of us just getting our needs met. But I knew that Anna wouldn't take it that way and that the day he was finished with her, there would be hell to pay. But on that day, I would do my best to not be around. I could see in her eyes she had Karl, that feeling of possession gave her a special glow, it was clear she lived for that right then, that she was happy in her way, the cruel way she had been taught by life and circumstances. Anna hadn't ever believed in human beings and that hadn't changed.

I'd like to say I had no part in what happened that day on tour, but I have to admit some of the fault is mine.

All the musicians were on the same plane except for Karl, who had left two days earlier so he could lock himself in his hotel room and rehearse. Obviously, on the flight, Anna and I sat as far away from each other as possible. Mark wasn't there, Mark was a nobody; his career only took off when his father died. These things happen, it's human to make an example out of someone, when that example is no longer there, we check to see who's waiting in line and we say, next.

When we arrived in Berlin, we didn't see Karl. We didn't know if he was in the same hotel, we were set to meet twenty-four hours before the concert for a sound check in the concert hall, and there he was. We rehearsed for barely half an hour, and then we each went our own way. As I was putting my violin in its case, he came over to me and said, come with me, please. And I turned and I didn't like what I saw in his eyes, it was need but not like the other times, not like in the past, it looked to me like he wasn't feeling well, and I quickly said yes and went with him to his hotel room. I didn't know he was ill; he never mentioned it to any of the musicians, including me, until that moment. He told me that a few days before the trip, he had spent two nights in the hospital with heart problems. Suddenly, he was drinking whiskey every time he made an extra effort, in other words, every time he had to conduct a concert. And he had an expression which I still hadn't identified with anything, and which I later understood was an expression of the pain of someone who needed medicine to keep going. It was an expression that scared me, even though I didn't know why at that point.

I followed him to his room. I knew that, after working together for those past couple of years, we had created an unbreakable bond, one that was different from the one he shared with other women, a bond that allowed us to share a certain intimacy, to understand each other with just a glance, and I knew that on this trip, even though he'd been sleeping with Anna, I was the one he most trusted. As much as Karl T. could trust anyone, that is, which wasn't much.

We went into his hotel room and he closed the door. What's wrong? I asked him immediately. Nothing, he said as he staggered over to the bed. I was frightened, you definitely don't look like nothing's wrong. I helped him to stretch out on the bed. He was breathing slowly, as if he was afraid he wouldn't have enough air otherwise. I just need a hug, you don't mind, do you? he said. He looked at me as if he was desperate for a candy. And at that moment I wondered if the great Karl T. had stage fright and wanted the support of a mother figure. I wondered a lot of things in a few seconds, and then I went over to him and hugged him, just as he had asked. And when his head was resting on my shoulder, I heard him say, this concert here is very important. If anything happens to me, he will conduct. I was shocked by his words, but Karl was referring to a name and phone number on a piece of paper he put into my hand. It was that of a well-known orchestra conductor, from Berlin, whom I was quite familiar with. But what are you saying, you are ill, do you want us to postpone the concert? I asked, frightened. No, no, he answered, lifting one hand, I just want the concert to go on, please, promise me. He looked at me as if he were asking me to promise that he would live. I made the promise, but then I asked him what was going on, whether he was feeling okay. I'm not well, he answered, and, I'm no spring chicken. He smiled a little as he said that, joking. I looked at him and, in that precise moment, I realized that Karl T. had gotten old. And not only that, but it looked like he was on his last legs. I didn't ask any more questions, he seemed tired.

Then there was a knock at the door. What do they want now? muttered Karl, thinking that it was the hotel staff. With a glance, he asked me to open up and I did. But it wasn't the bellboy, no. It was Anna, standing there with one of those expressions that say it all. *Oh, no*, I thought, closing my eyes for a fleeting moment.

Obviously, it was too late for me to hide. Excuse me, my mistake, she said. And she disappeared.

I closed the door gently and sighed. Then I walked over to him. He looked at me with fear in his eyes for a moment, but then he asked, where were we? I hugged him again, not without some concern, because I wondered what that twisted girl was capable of.

Anyway, it was odd that Anna caught us together on the only day we were alone together without making love. Stranger things have happened. I left once I was sure that Karl was okay and just wanted to sleep. I was worried something might happen to him that night and I offered to stay, but he assured me there was no need. I placed a note by the telephone, where I had written, very large, my room number. Then I left.

The next day, our conductor was fresh as a rose. As if nothing had happened. And we performed the concert in Berlin, and he left very early the next day for Vienna, while all the musicians remained in the German capital for one more day.

Anna

It's raining. It's raining and the leaves on the ground look like plates holding water. And the water holds more bits and pieces of my soul. It's here in the river, and in the lake in Barcelona. I've got bits of my soul everywhere; it's odd how something so intangible can divide itself up like that. But I can't gather up those pieces, I've tried, but there's no way. It's not the water's fault anyway. It's everyone's fault, everyone who broke my soul and threw it into the lake by the house and said, go on, sweetheart, go find it, and if it's broken, piece it back together. I never did piece it back together. At first I tried to and then, when it no longer hurt, I let it go, if my soul wanted to be in the water, all broken up in bits, then so be it. It wasn't my fault, it was everyone else's. Including Mark, who won't even let me into his dressing room. It's everyone's fault.

It's very dark. Night had already fallen when we arrived; here the days are short and the scant sunlight doesn't last long. It's still raining. I'd like to take a walk, dragging my feet through the puddles, letting them get soaked. I'd like to, but I have to perform soon, in presentable shoes. Everyone has gone back inside for the beginning of the second part. It's the second part in every way. The second part of the comedy of my life, with a human being deep inside me and water falling constantly but without making a sound, as if trying to go unnoticed. The Berlin natives, who are used to this weather, walk quickly beneath umbrellas of every color. And I'm thinking about when I found out that Teresa and Karl were lovers.

I think it was the last time my soul broke into more pieces. That was when I realized that Teresa, who had been a point of reference in my life, really lived to hurt me. That she must not have any other goals in life. When I caught them red-handed in that hotel room, in this very city, I made a colossal effort to make it look like I couldn't care less. Teresa's apologetic expression, as if she were innocence itself, as if playing at its being some misunderstanding, was what incensed me more than anything. I left there as quickly as I could, wondering how she could be so nasty, so twisted, how I could have ever trusted her. It seems, as kids, we can fall for anything.

That day, when I got to the banks of the Spree, I could barely breathe. The water flowed peacefully, but I was gasping for air. I screamed, leaning over the railing above those abundant waters, and then I started to breathe quickly, mixing gulps of air with sobs that came out all at once, the sobs of an entire life, sobs of truth, over that woman who was determined to finish me off, over that woman who is about to play Bach's *Concerto for Two Violins* with me onstage. I'm sure the evil bitch seduced Karl, tricking him somehow to get him into that hotel room, I'm sure she saw that there was something between us and she thought, *well, I'll snatch him away, and leave Anna alone, with nothing and no one.*

The world is difficult for some people, and I was one of them; the hawk-nosed music teacher had been right, my fate was to live *en souffrant*—until I decided that enough was enough, one day ten years ago, sobbing above the River Spree. I wondered how Teresa had managed to get the spot as the other violin in the Bach concert, how she had managed to get close to me again, to find another way to hurt me. And when I'd first seen her, I thought it was just a coincidence, a perverse coincidence but a coincidence just the same. But, of course, after everything that's happened, I no longer believe in coincidences, it's not possible, there has to be some trick, and the trick is Teresa, who won't miss a chance to screw me over. I saw that clearly that day above the Spree. And that was when I said enough is enough, I wasn't going to play the fool anymore, I would never again be so naïve. I wished I had the Stainer with me then, but I didn't. I had just given it to Karl. To Karl, who had promised to marry me when we got back from tour, to Karl who I believed was mine.

I had believed that Mama was mine, and Teresa, and Papa, and Karl. And none of them were, they had all deceived me. But now Mark will be mine, because of this baby inside me. And now I have the violin to flaunt in front of Teresa. She doesn't even glance at it, she acts like she doesn't care that I'm touring the world with an instrument that had been hers since she was a child, according to what she told me. One day I asked her who had given it to her, it seemed weird that someone would give a little girl a Stainer, and Teresa told me that she had found it. I gave a start. What, and you didn't return it? It had been abandoned, she said quickly, then changed the subject. I don't know what she meant by that, but some time later, when she did all that to me, when she stole Karl from me, I thought that it might be a good idea to discover where she'd found it, who she'd stolen it from, because obviously no one just leaves a Stainer on a park bench like an old sweater. Maybe at first I'd half-believed the story of the abandoned violin, but years later, when the scales fell from my eyes, I saw the truth and I understood that Teresa had stolen the violin. But after thinking over the idea of finding out whose it really was, I let it go because then the violin was mine again, and if I discovered its true owner I could lose it again.

I remembered that, when that happened, when I caught Karl with that nasty bitch; it was right before the concert, the evening before. And I needed that time to recover, there by the banks of the Spree. I wanted to show up for the concert with a clean face and not a single tear, and it wasn't easy for me to pull off. I can't say I performed my best that day, I had trouble concentrating, and I felt as if there were an electrical current between me and Teresa, and I struggled to turn my focus the other way, toward Karl, toward the man who had promised to marry me. And then, in the middle of the concert, during the second movement, I said to myself, he will marry me, he's promised to and that was the only way I could hurt Teresa. That was my best revenge.

But we didn't get married. Karl boarded the plane the next day, while we were sightseeing in his native city. And we were at the Brandenburg Gate listening to the explanations of a tour guide when the manager's phone rang. He stayed behind while we kept walking, and then he called out to us and we turned. I can still remember the image of that small man, silhouetted in the back-light, with his cell phone in his hand, when he said to us, he's dead. No one asked who. Everyone knew, I don't know why; we all knew he was talking about Karl.

That was the end of the sightseeing, that was the end of the tour, and that was the end of my future. But I thought that I had lost the violin—and it turns out that, no, that was the one thing I managed not to lose.

Maria

Many people attended Mr. Karl's funeral. The ceremony was led by a man who wasn't a priest, but it was almost as if he were, anyway; he bid farewell to the deceased. And they played the most beautiful music. Miss Teresa was near the front, crying. I didn't see Miss Anna. And Mr. Mark was also crying, sitting in the very first row. He asked me to sit with him and at first I said no, but he was crying so much and finally he said, don't leave me alone, Maria, and I understood that he needed me, so I sat there with him. Even though, honestly, I didn't feel it was my place.

My heart was shattered. That death had destroyed my life, and I knew it would be very hard for me to recover from it. I had climbed a mountain little by little, a very high mountain, and when it seemed I was just reaching its peak, it turned out I wasn't going to make it. I didn't want to look at the coffin; when I closed my eyes, the image of Mr. Karl appeared, images I knew so well: him scooping up spoonfuls of hot chocolate and laughing the way he did; him gazing at me as I played the song about the peasant girl and the shepherd; images of the man who had written me that letter, and even of the one who entertained so many women on that black leather sofa. And then I opened my eyes and I saw that wooden box. It couldn't be, the man inside there couldn't be the one I remembered.

Miss Anna hadn't gone to the burial, but she did come to the house four days later. It was the same Miss Anna of today, ten years younger. She was pretty, and she still is, but she's getting too many lines on her face, and she has two prominent wrinkles on her forehead from that worried expression she makes when she plays. Mrs. Anna has become scary, like the stepmother in *Snow White* that I would sometimes hear the nannies in the park telling kids about. But today, despite her scariness, even though she's an evil witch, she looks very elegant. She's wearing a long black dress with a plunging neckline, and I've noticed that all the men are looking to see if they can catch a glimpse of her breasts. It's funny, years ago I would have been shocked by the mere thought. And now, it makes me laugh.

I'm not wearing a revealing dress, but I do look elegant. It's a shame my stomach is so bad, that I don't feel well, because today could be one of those days to hold my head up high and feel the eyes on me, even though my feet are dragging somewhat because I'm tired and too old to be wearing heels. It would be great to just walk on solid ground, it gives you the feeling that you know where you are, that you are in charge of your own fate. But no, with these high heels, no matter how low they are, they only let you walk on tiptoe, and you don't know what galaxy you're in. Not to mention how uncomfortable they are. I like my dress though, I went shopping one day to see what I could find and I chose a brown dress that looks quite good on me. Mr. Mark said, wow, don't you look elegant, Maria, and I puffed up like a peacock. He said it when Miss Anna wasn't around, of course, because no ever says anything like that in front of her.

Miss Anna came over ten years ago and said, hello, I've come to pick up a violin that I left the last time I was rehearsing here with Karl. I looked at her and a shiver ran through my entire body: When Miss Anna started to come to the house, Mr. Karl had told me, that woman has the devil in her, and I swear it's true.

Now it's time for me to get up and do my job. The job I came here to do.

Teresa

I just saw Maria over there, in a corner. It seems like she scurried off when she saw me watching her. What in the world is she doing here? Isn't she supposed to be sitting in the audience listening to the concert? I don't even want to know. Maybe she's looking for someone, but if so it's not me, because otherwise she wouldn't have scampered off when she saw me.

This music brings back so many memories of Karl. I think, in that period before his death, he had come to think of me as some sort of mother figure, or like an older sister. We hadn't been physical for some time, I guess because he had enough of that with Anna, and yet, since I was probably the only woman who hadn't gotten upset with him when the business on the sofa ended, he must have had a special love for me. The truth is that I didn't have it in me anymore, I had loved Maties so much that I couldn't love any other man that same way again. So, from the very beginning, I understood the whole thing with Karl as a life experience and nothing more than that. The thing is that, when Anna found out, it was all over between us. In fact, the next morning, in the light of day and before the Berlin concert, I thought that it had just been that Karl needed some human warmth before the performance. Later, I realized that he needed more than warmth. He needed a doctor. But, of course, I had no idea at the time. Only his son and Maria knew about his heart problems, and they were both home in Barcelona. And as far as Karl was concerned, the music came first and his health wasn't even a close second.

I didn't find out about his death until after the others. I hadn't gone sightseeing because I was sure that Anna would be there, and I didn't feel like seeing her. I thought that she and I could talk some other time, if at all. Maybe we never would because she would restrain herself, the way I had restrained myself the day before in the hotel, not going after her because I didn't want another door slammed in my face, like the one in the hospital; I didn't want that to happen to me ever again. And also because, it bears mentioning, I was starting to think that she deserved it all, that maybe Anna had to start to realize that, despite her own difficulties in life, other people had problems too and we didn't deserve to be treated that way.

No one told me what had happened until we met up to fly to Vienna. There, in the hotel lobby, only those who hadn't heard showed up, the ones who didn't know that the flight had been cancelled and we were going back to Barcelona the next day. How strange, there's barely anyone here, commented a young woman from the orchestra. Yeah, said another, but, of course, none of us knew that the only ones there were those who hadn't gone sightseeing, because everyone on the tour already knew. I remember those impressions and thoughts right before the manager dropped the bombshell, as if it had just happened yesterday. Then he came down and told us. And I was shocked stiff. The others were, too; Karl was their conductor, they had played for many years in the orchestra he had assembled, but it affected me in a more personal way, of course. I couldn't keep myself from bursting into tears while the manager explained how it had happened. A few of the young women also shed a tear, and all of us, in general, were unsure what to do or what to say. The manager announced our departure time for the next day and disappeared, and I took my suitcase back up to my hotel room. There I cried for a good long while. From the depths of my heart, though, a little voice told me, thank goodness, Teresa, that you didn't throw yourself into it the way you had with Maties. Because if you had, this would have sunk you forever. I did decide that, from that point on, I would be particularly careful with men, because it seemed obvious that, once I got involved with them, they met a tragic end.

The return to Barcelona was a sad, silent one. I didn't even look at Anna, I didn't want to have anything to do with her, I wasn't up for her sarcastic games or mocking looks. I stayed as far away from her as I could and, once I was home, one thought eased the pain I was feeling, which was that while I might see her at the funeral, I would never have to see her again after that. Never again.

And I didn't even see her at the burial, I don't think she came. I'm not sure, because there were so many people there, but my guess is that she wasn't there. And, oddly, the only women at the ceremony were the women from his orchestra. I alone of his lovers was there. All the rest were men. I figured that all of his former lovers had ended up angry with him. I was surprised to find out that he was much older than I had thought. You held up well, Karl, I thought as a silent tear slid down my cheek, to think I thought you were only eight or nine years older than me. And then, in a flash, I calculated the gap between him and Anna. My God, you seduced a child, I recriminated that silent coffin. And, for a few seconds, I felt sorry for her again, for that unlucky, abandoned, fragile girl. Just for a few seconds.

Sometimes I think about how Karl was. He didn't think of his sexual relationships as romantic affairs, no, Karl lived in another world and had no idea what was going on in this one. For Karl, a female musician who played with him had to take the music as far as possible, and that including getting involved with him. It sounds strange to say, but I'm sure that he thought it was the most normal, natural thing in the world, and he never meant to hurt anyone. He lived in his own world.

But Anna didn't live in his world, and she never could have. She is of our world, and she does try to cause as much pain as she can. When, a few years later, I went to see Mark, I discovered that Anna was two steps ahead of me, and not only that, but it seemed that Mark was really taken with her. I remember thinking, in resignation, *This girl is never going to change.* Mark lived in an apartment near where Karl had. That house belonged to the government, he explained to me, and they had let him use it when they granted him political asylum but it didn't belong to him. But when I saw Mark's apartment, I thought that all the money Karl had earned over his lifetime must not have been the government's, no. It was obvious that his son had inherited a tidy sum.

I went back to the conservatory and my quartet. We had

worked and played in different places. Almost every week, we would go out and we enjoyed making music together. What more did I want? That was the life I had chosen from the day I found the magic violin at the dump.

I still play with the same quartet, although less frequently. There came a moment when I'd had enough of all the traveling, a moment when I felt my age, or something like it, weighing on my shoulders. I also had no desire to work closely with any particular conductor the way I had with Karl, and I said no when I had offers. One of the ones who came looking for me was Mark. He had begun to make a name for himself, but I've always thought that he continuted to bear his father's. Because Mark was an excellent cellist, but as a conductor I would never place him among the best. I was very pleased to see him again, but I immediately said no; I don't remember what excuse I gave. Working with Mark surely would have meant running into Anna all the time. And that was the last thing I wanted.

I lived alone, and I lived quite well, because I didn't live in the neighborhood by the park but in a different part of the city where the rents weren't so astronomical. And one day I ran into Maria.

And another day, I saw a television interview with Anna about her Stainer, the violin that had lost its magic when it fell into the hands of that musical robot. Good Lord, and to think that I was once her teacher and I was unable to teach her to put anything more than speed into her music. Anna, on TV, showed off her trophy, explaining how rare it was and how difficult it had been for her to acquire. I was eating almonds as I watched the show, and I stopped chewing to exclaim, spontaneously: Sweet Mother of God, what nerve!

Mark

The first part went well. And the second sounds amazing so far. All our rehearsing paid off. The audience is silent, and I wipe the sweat from my forehead with my white handkerchief, like my father used to. It has to be white, always, it's more elegant that way. That was what the great Karl T. said, and whether out of genetics or admiration, Mark T. says the same thing.

Be careful with your heart, these things are hereditary, said Maria, before we said goodbye ten years ago. She said it with tears in her eyes. The poor thing hated to leave, but in my new apartment, even though it was large, we would have been on top of each other. I would ask you to come iron and tidy things up, but now you have money and you don't want to clean apartments anymore, right? She was quick to say, oh, yes, Mr. Mark, of course I'll come. Mark, I corrected her with a smile, and she said, sorry, Mark. Maria was so beloved to me, and she still is, she brings back such memories of my father, they lived together for forty years and knew each other inside and out. My father wasn't easy to live with, he was a strange man, who only lived for music, and no one understood him. I'm not even sure I ever came to understand him myself, in all the years I spent by his side.

When the will was read, I was left without a doubt that he and Maria had understood each other well. It was a will that he had amended a few years earlier, when I had come to Barcelona. So I was also included. If it weren't for me, he would have left everything to Maria. Since my father had everything paid for, he was able to save every penny he earned, which was a lot. So Maria was able to buy herself an apartment and quit working. And I also bought an apartment, but I didn't stop working. In fact, that was when I started to get a ton of work, mostly things my father couldn't do. All of a sudden, I got all kinds of offers, I was traveling all over, like before, but now not to study or perform, but to direct, with the orchestra my father had left orphaned.

When I met Anna I told her about Maria and what my father had left her, and she didn't understand it. How could you let your father do that, you're his only son, how could you not care that he left half of his fortune to a maid? Anna's take on it left me shocked, especially when I saw how strongly she felt about it. Her eyes were flashing with anger as if it were her own father. I took a long, hard look at her, sure that it wasn't a question of money, because she had plenty. What could it have been, then? I don't know. What I do know is that what had happened really didn't bother me; it seemed appropriate to me that Maria should inherit a good part of my father's money. Well, I would have been upset if I hadn't gotten anything, sure, I answered Anna, but I have enough with what he left me. It seems like a lot to me. Besides, the most important part of the inheritance was the last name, it suddenly opened up so many doors for me that allowed me to make music, my music.

Anna came into my life about five years ago. I had only seen her once before, at my father's house on one of the very rare times when I was there. Her presence made a real impact on me, it's true, but I didn't say a word to her. And five years ago, I called her for a concert and she showed me how she was capable of playing. She drove me wild, both the way she played and the way she was. When I saw her enter the room where we were rehearsing, her hips swaying and that gaze that was so deep and so dark, I felt lost and I had to make a superhuman effort to concentrate on what I was doing. I think that she could tell, because she seemed amenable. Right then, and from that moment on.

And now I don't know how to get rid of her. I know that it's not nice to even think this, but that woman is suffocating me. I feel obliged to ask her to do all the violin solos, and she does play very well, but there are also other violinists that I'd like to try. And she never lets me walk alone, I can't take two steps without having her at my side. It's like I'm always dragging along a complicated burden. And every time there are other people around, she comes over to take my hand. All the love, all the tenderness that I wanted to give her in the beginning has vanished. There is none of it left, nothing of those first days in her house, when I would walk her home after rehearsal and she would say, come on in, I won't bite. But it was a lie, she ate me up, and I liked it, it drove me wild. I don't know what she did to me, but she had me blinded. And now she'll come out and play Bach with Teresa, whom she loathes and wants to see fail. What is it with you and Teresa? I asked her one day. Nothing, she answered quickly. Well, you are always attacking her, and she seems like a good person. Then Anna got up suddenly, as if the button on a spring she had inside had been pressed, turning her so terrifying that even I was scared. Don't be taken in by appearances, she said, pointing to the heavens with that tiny, decisive nose of hers. And I laughed a little, at that point I still found her funny, I still loved her, I still believed her.

Tonight, after the concert, I'm going to tell her that it's over. I've made up my mind.

Anna

Now as I'm about to go onstage, with the scent of rain that's reached my brain, now that I feel my adrenaline rising, I remember the day I saw her again, just like now, before heading out on stage. In that concert hall you could see the audience from the wings, and I looked out at the seats and I saw her there, waiting for my entrance. My jaw dropped. She didn't know that I had seen her, she wasn't looking at me just then.

Now that I have Teresa and her violin in reach, now that I can feel her resigned, silent presence, her loathsome presence, I remember the shock of glimpsing that other woman out there in the audience, before I went onstage. It took a titanic effort to recover. I had to cling to the Stainer, the Stainer that I had gone to get back from the maid, who looked like she was planning on keeping it. I clutched it tightly, and I closed my eyes and I said to myself, this can't be. And I opened them again, and yes, it could be, she was still there in the audience, attentively watching the performance. And then our eyes met and I thought I wouldn't be able to play. I had confronted a lot of things in this life, but that one was too much.

Mark enters to roaring applause. He wipes the sweat from his forehead with his little white handkerchief and looks at us with a half-smile: "Okay, ladies, the stage is all yours."

I see that Teresa steps aside to let me pass, so I paint a smile on my lips and make my entrance. The orchestra stands up, the crowd claps. The applause is like a balsam for my skin, which is too thin and delicate. Luckily, I have the spotlights and the warmth of the audience, luckily, I've had it all these years, because some things are hard to overcome.

What are you doing here? I asked when she hobbled into my dressing room, after a couple of knocks on the door that made me fear the worst. She smiled, I saw that you saw me, she said. And it was a twisted smile, a smile filled with wrinkles that had lost its youthful charm. You've gotten old, I blurted out mercilessly. She took it in stride, we all get old, she said. And then she added, I'm truly sorry about what happened, I didn't want to leave like that, but your father forced me to. I arched my brows, everyone has their own version of the story, I said. He's dead, isn't he? she said. Yes, years ago, I answered. And then I asked her, what do you want? She paused briefly before answering, nothing, I just wanted to see you. And she added, you play very well, and you didn't even like the violin. *It was the only thing I had,* I shouted inside my own head. Well, now you've seen me, I said out loud, abruptly. She kept asking questions, are you married? do you have children? I didn't know if I should answer, and finally I said, I live with a man. I didn't tell her that it was the conductor of the concert she had just seen. Then, she seemed to find the way to tell me what she'd wanted to, look, your father didn't take you, because he said that children should be with their mothers. I was silent, I understood less and less this cruel game of making foolish remarks that hit me like a punch in the stomach; now that I was over it, here she comes with her drivel. I looked at her and said, why couldn't you have each had me part-time? What you're saying is nonsense, Mama.

I had said Mama. It had been so many years since I'd used the word. She sighed, he didn't want to because he said that you would have wanted to just live with him. As I applied my lipstick, I thought, *He may have been right.* My mother finished her speech, I went to live abroad with a man, and now that I'm back, I try to come to all your concerts. I've also attended some of your concerts on tour, in Paris, Madrid, Lyon. I applied more lipstick and then licked my lips before saying, please, leave. I said it softly, very softly. She turned tail and I watched her—old, so very old—heading slowly to the door and opening it. Before she disappeared, all she said was, forgive me.

So I found myself alone and I began to tremble like a leaf. The last thing I needed was to worry about running into Mama at every concert from now on. Then Mark came in and saw me sitting, staring at the floor, and asked me what was wrong. I'm not feeling very well, I said, I don't know, I'm dizzy. It'll pass. Mark and I had been living in the best of worlds for some time, he and I and the Stainer, in that apartment uptown, where the plants in the gardens delicately kiss the foundations of beautifully designed buildings. Sometimes, I would go for a walk to the lake to see if my soul was there, so I could tell it that I no longer needed it. But after seeing Mama for the first time, I did need my soul, and when

I went looking for it, I found it had left once again. Suddenly, I had lost my peace and tranquility. I had Mark and the Stainer, but they weren't enough. And then came a period of a lot of work, and at each concert I looked for Mama, and I knew she was there but she never came to see me after the show. And then I got pneumonia, and they tore the violin from my hands and forced me to get some bed rest. Mark had to hire a substitute for me in the concerts and I couldn't stand seeing another woman put in my place and I asked Mark to let me do it, that I would do it well, that even sick I could do it, and I started to practice every evening when he wasn't there. I would grab the Stainer and play and play with all the rage I could muster. I was imagining Mama watching the concert and watching the other violinist who Mark said played so well, who maybe Mama liked even better than her own daughter, maybe she was there for that violinist.

And one evening, I waited for Mark in my pajamas and with the Stainer in my hand. My whole being was aboil, but I couldn't bear to think that he was rehearsing with another violinist. I sat waiting until he opened the door, and then I put the violin on my shoulder and I began to play. I played Tartini's *Il trillo del diavolo*. I played it with a feeling that I'd never had before, and even more so when I saw Mark approach and stand watching me in surprise. I put a passion into it that wasn't soul but pure passion. I played for two long minutes, carried along by the fever or the devil himself, I'm not sure which. At the last moment, before falling to the floor, I thought that knowing that Mama was trailing me had me all shook up.

They took me to the hospital, and, later, Mark took me to a spa for ten days. Ten days without the violin. I didn't miss my instrument because I had my man, who only lived to make me happy.

Now he's here at the front of the stage about to mark our entrances. First comes Teresa and then me, on the fifth bar. In fact when this concert is over, I'll never have to see Teresa again. That will be the end of it. I place the violin on my shoulder and, when it's my turn, I begin my melody. And then, for some mysterious reason, a strange, deformed sound emerges from inside the Stainer; and all of a sudden, everything comes unmoored.

Maria

I didn't stay at the concert to see what happened when it came time for her to play. When the applause began for the piece before the violin duet, before the two women came on stage to play Bach, I just got up and left. Well, I got up best I could and walked across the entire row, saying, excuse me, excuse me, and everyone looked at me strangely because they couldn't understand what I was saying and because I was stumbling over everyone in this long dress that almost reaches my feet. Now I've made it out, down the stairs and to the theater's side entrance. Outside, everything is dark. And there, pure silence, the audience is in the great hall, there where Mrs. Anna must be wanting to tear her hair out because her violin isn't sounding like it should. I look at the coat check woman, like before, who doesn't understand me but lets out a little oh! when she sees me and points to the case by her side, half hidden among the coats.

"Yes, exactly . . . I'll take my coat and the instrument . . . thank you."

She understands me perfectly and hands me both things. *She must be tired,* she must be thinking, *I've had enough of this lady, with her I'll collect the case and now I'll check it again*—I smile at her and nod as if to say thank you and goodbye.

I can barely stand, my stomach feels like a pressure cooker but not because I need to use the bathroom, actually I haven't eaten a thing all day. It's just hurting horribly. But I don't care, I smile. At my age, even pain brings a smile. I cover up and go outside. I look back and see a brightly lit sign that reads *Staatsoper im Schiller Theatre.* I hold my breath and think how I don't really know what it means, but the letters make an impact because they are so large and bright. I didn't notice them yesterday, and I didn't notice them today when we arrived. Oh, because it was still light out and we came in a cab, I say to myself. I can't see much, but I can tell the ground is wet. Yet it's stopped raining.

It rained the day that I ran into Miss Teresa on my street. It was the street where my new house is, the apartment I bought in a more humble neighborhood than the one where Mr. Karl lived. Mr. Mark, on the other hand, stayed close, and I would go over to his apartment to tidy up, in exchange for a small salary and the chance to chat for a little while with someone who appreciated me. But sometimes Mr. Mark wasn't there because he was increasingly popular and had more and more concerts; he was starting to seem like Mr. Karl in that way, but only in that way, because he will never be like his father, and he will never make the music his father did.

When I found out that he had left me so much money, I didn't even care. I didn't care about anything, not a single thing, except for the fact that Mr. Karl had suddenly disappeared from my life completely. First, it seemed that it was all just so unfair, and then I felt lonely. After forty years of his company, I no longer had anyone. All I had was money, but I didn't really care about the inheritance. I realized that I was doing everything, going everywhere, with my eyes constantly wet with tears. There was nothing I could do to get rid of them, the tears had stuck to my eyes, they didn't want to go inside, they only wanted to flow out. I felt sad, sad, sad. Every once in a while I would kiss the letter he had left me, and in those first days, when no one else was around, I would play the German songs on the Stainer, especially the one about the peasant girl and the shepherd. And I would think, *Oh, if only Mr. Karl had told me earlier what he'd told me in the letter.*

Until Miss Anna showed up and took the violin away. I couldn't keep her from going into the piano room, just like I had never been able to when she would come by the house. It was my bad luck that the Stainer was in the room just then because I'd been playing it, and the piano room had the best soundproofing in the whole house, Mr. Karl had had special walls put in so the neighbors wouldn't complain. Miss Anna headed straight there, grabbed the Stainer, and asked me, where is the case? in the haughtiest voice I'd ever heard. But, Miss, the violin is not yours. Of course it's mine, anyone who knows me will say that I play this violin, I'll prove it to you anytime you'd like. But you gave it to Mr. Karl, he told me, I exclaimed. Miss Anna looked at me for a moment with doubt in her eyes, but then she started to laugh and said, what nonsense, why would I give the Stainer to Karl, don't make me laugh.

I was desperate and I didn't know what to do. I wanted to go find the letter and show her the proof that violin was no longer Mr. Karl's but mine now, but I was held back by the rest of the contents of the letter, because if I showed Miss Anna the part of the letter where it said that he was giving me the violin and that he had gotten it in exchange for promising to marry her, I would have had to show her the entire page, and I wasn't willing to do that, at least not then. So, after a few seconds of thinking it over, I told myself that it was best not to do anything, to just let it go. She saw that I was giving up the fight over the instrument, and then she seized the moment to say, so, are you going to give me the case or do I have to walk through the streets with it like this?

All of a sudden, I hated her. I had never felt anything like that before and I didn't enjoy the feeling, but at that moment there was nothing I could do about it. I went to my room, grabbed the case and brought it to her, holding back my tears, which were tears of rage right then, not of sadness. She placed the instrument inside, and, without even a word of thanks, she said farewell and left. Then I really did burst into tears.

They didn't last long, though. At least not the tears over the violin. The others, the ones over Mr. Karl, didn't last long either, on the outside, but they were flowing inside me for a very long time, and there was no way I could stop the flow. Crying inside had never happened to me before either; it was like hating Miss Anna, which gradually faded, because I understood that such a negative feeling could only hurt me and so it would be stupid to hold on to it. But the tears for Mr. Karl, ay, those were harder for me to get past, and they soaked my insides as if they were vinegar because they burned holes in my stomach and everywhere, and not like now, when it also feels like I've got vinegar in my stomach, but in a different way that no doctor could heal.

When Mr. Mark and I left the house by the lake, he asked me if I wanted to take anything with me. I asked him if I could take the violin, the other one, the student violin. He always played it, I lied. Oh, really, and I thought he had given up the violin. You didn't spend much time at home, Mr. Mark, I mean Mark, I said. That's true, he conceded with a sad smile. And isn't there anything else you want? he asked. I hesitated for a moment, well, yes, there is something I'd like to have, but I'm not sure I'll be able to because it's very heavy. Mr. Mark arched his eyebrows as he waited. Beethoven, I said quickly. Then Mr. Mark started laughing, that's a good one, Maria, you are such a card, I don't know if they'll let us, but we'll do everything we can, I doubt they'll raise a fuss over a plaster bust.

They didn't. In fact, they had placed Beethoven there as a nod to Mr. Karl, but surely if they wanted to sell or rent that house, they'd have to move it, because it occupied a space that any normal family would rather use for a small table or one of those lamps that people keep in their entryways. And so Beethoven came to my new house, to my small apartment. He didn't fit in my entryway, not even in my kitchen, so I had to give him a room, the other one that wasn't my bedroom, because there were only two. And there he was in the middle and I would dust him every day, and at first I would just say *gut'n Tag*, but then I started to tell him more things and to talk to him about Mr. Karl, and I read him the letter that I now carry in my pocket, and not just once but I read it to him a thousand times, and every time I read it to him, there were tears. Mine, not Beethoven's, because he was made of plaster, and I had thought he was made of stone but no; he wasn't that hard. But anyway, he was cold and he gave me quite a look, and he must have been deaf, too—because they say even the real one couldn't hear a thing. And then I would pick up the violin and tune it best I could without a piano, but I discovered that, if I listened to any radio station that played classical music, I could tune it; it came naturally, I quickly found the A, and then I could play the German songs, especially the one about the peasant girl and the shepherd, but I cried so much that I decided to stop for a while and not play it anymore, at least until some time had passed.

At first everything was sad and dark. The apartment was so small, and I felt as if my breathing was constricted. Once a week I went over to Mr. Mark's place and kept things in order, even though I didn't need the money, thanks to Mr. Karl's inheritance. Mr. Karl had never spent anything, he hadn't even paid for the Stainer, because it was a gift from his father, and I didn't have many expenses because I lived alone—so, with what he had left me, I could live forever, if I wanted to.

When I left Mr. Mark's house, I always went by the park and the lake with its still waters where lilies or their beds of leaves floated. And I would close my eyes for a moment to smell the green scent, and I listened to the lullaby of the tinkling poplar leaves and the shouts of the children playing in the afternoon, like those other kids that Miss Teresa used to watch so long ago, the ones that always got away from her.

Miss Teresa came to my apartment one day because I ran into her right out front, and it was raining. She smiled at me and asked me how I was doing. We got to talking about Mr. Karl. Fortunately, it was years since his death, and I could talk about him normally, without crying. I invited her up to my apartment; it just came out suddenly like that, because it would have been rude not to and then have her see me enter the building. She was carrying a bottle of cava that someone had just given her. We'll drink it together, she said happily. And we went upstairs, and I took her past the room with Beethoven and the violin to avoid having to explain, and I had her come into the little dining room, and she exclaimed, it's very nice, and she asked me if I still saw Mr. Mark. And I said no, not anymore, because it was true, two days earlier I had been let go.

Miss Teresa and I had a couple of glasses of cava. I had learned many things at Mr. Karl's house and the other homes where I had worked before that, and one of those things was that it was important to be prepared for guests and have a few glasses always at the ready, because you never knew what could happen and who might come over. Then I thought that I should have had some cava on hand, but fortunately that time Miss Teresa had brought it with her. Why is that? she asked me when I told her I no longer saw Mr. Mark. I sighed, well, now Miss Anna spends a lot of time there, and Miss Anna doesn't like me very much, you know. I didn't tell Miss Teresa that Mr. Mark had given me a phone number where I could reach him if I needed to and that he had told me to keep the keys to the house, and that he had apologized a thousand times.

Miss Teresa took a sip of cava and coughed a little. Anna is a complicated person, she said in a vague tone. She finished her drink and poured some more. I didn't stop her, I just drank two glasses and she drank all the rest. And, when it had all gone to her head, she solved the mystery of the Stainer for me.

Oh, all of a sudden I can't breathe. I can't move. Everything is dark and no one can see me, here in this square filled with slippery, wet tiles in front of the theater. Finally, with much effort, I manage to put one foot in front of the other, but it's obvious I won't be able to walk much farther. Holy Beloved Virgin of the Macarena, now I clearly see that I won't make it back to Barcelona.

Teresa

My God, that was terrible. The audience didn't realize that the Stainer wasn't the Stainer, but they could tell that something was wrong because all three of us—Anna, Mark, and I—were in a state of shock when we heard the instrument. And we played two bars and then Anna stopped. You could see she wanted to go on but couldn't, she hadn't entered on time, it seemed something was holding her back, that her fingers wouldn't move, that she couldn't press down on the strings, that she couldn't make the bow move. It seemed she couldn't do anything until she snapped out of her shock. Then Mark had had to stop everything. There was a deathly silence in the concert hall. The orchestra, if they had noticed anything, they hadn't shown it, but the three of us were petrified. Mark looked at Anna. And Anna, red as a beet, looked at the violin, which looked exactly like the Stainer, but wasn't the Stainer. And I looked at the instrument too, but not openly because I realized that we had to do something to save the situation. And, luckily, my *partenaire* hadn't peered through the f-hole to see if Stainer's signature was there, because that would have made us look really, really bad. She had simply stopped, perplexed. It had all been a matter of seconds, and then Mark had saved the day, turning toward the audience and, with a smile on his lips, said, for those of you who don't know, he always did it this way, with a false entrance like the one in the Blue Danube at the New Year's concert. The crowd laughed and applauded. Then Mark turned and gave us both a look that said, Stainer or no, we are going to give our best concert. And we did, forgetting about the fact that Anna wasn't playing the Stainer. To be fair, I have to say that she bounced back exceptionally well. The fact that she controls her emotions so well had helped her to maintain her composure and play with a new, strange violin the way she would have with the Stainer or any violin she'd known all her life. I was impressed. When we finished, we were showered with applause, and I thought that she was the one who deserved it. That day, she had more than earned her recognition from the audience. We took a bow, they brought us some flowers, and now we've just gone offstage while the orchestra takes their seats.

"What happened?!" I ask once we're backstage, looking at Anna's violin.

"I don't know—" she says, looking at it as well.

She seems sincere, completely sincere. She doesn't know what happened, just like Mark and me. But he is still holding the baton and says, "Come on, let's go back out before the applause dies down."

We paint a smile on our lips and go out onto the stage. Sometimes you have to do that in life, paint on a smile and go out. Here, there are warming spotlights, but outside it's cold. And then you find yourself very alone, like I did after Karl's death, despite returning to the Conservatory and the quartet. Because Karl had symbolized something more to me than the sexual release of the early days. He wasn't like Maties, there wasn't that unbridled passion and that mutual vision of life together, that feeling that I'd found my soul mate. No, it was just that Karl, the great orchestra conductor, had captured my soul, that soul he said I put so much of into my playing. And he hadn't even heard me play the magic violin, that magic violin that God knows where it's gone to now, perhaps into the hands of someone who knows how to work its spell. My violin that glowed in the garbage heap; who knows if right now it's at some other dump?

I won't ever say where I found that violin, I said. What violin? asked Maria. Oh, the one that Anna has now, the Stainer. I looked at her for a moment, and even though I had drunk almost an entire bottle of cava on my own, I suddenly realized that I was talking to Maria about something she could never understand. That no matter how fond I was of her and what a charming person she was, that she must not be able to tell the difference between a Stainer and an Olivera. Sorry, I said drinking the last sip in my glass, it's a kind of strange story, you know, Anna's violin used to be mine. She looked at me as if she'd never seen me before. Go on, tell me, she said eagerly, as if she were very interested. We were in her house, we had run into each other on the street and I was carrying a bottle of cava, and I thought it would be better to drink it with her than by myself, because lately I'd been reduced to that. And Maria and I had always gotten along, she was very kind, so we had a nice time remembering Karl and talking about how Barcelona had changed.

Then she told me that she wouldn't be going to Mark's house any-more because Anna had pretty much moved in, and so I ended up telling her my story about the dump. I had never told it to anyone before, but considering Maria's background, she was the perfect candidate to understand that at the dump you can find fascinating things. Even if she didn't know what a Stainer was. So I started by explaining to her about the Stainer and why that violin was so valuable. I told her a bit about the luthier, who was Tyrolean and had lived in the 17th century, and I also explained, in the simplest words I could, that the instruments he had made were special, that they had a special sound and that through the f-hole you could read his signature, Jacobus Stainer, and the date of the violin's con-struction.

Ours is from 1672, I explained. I continued with some addi-tional facts, things I remembered about the instrument maker, oh, and at the start of the 19th century, his instruments were considered better than the Italians'. Than the Italians'? She repeated, looking at me with wide eyes. Yes, the ones from Cremona. Stradivarius, Amati, you know. But she must not have known, because she made a confused expression, and so I explained myself better, yes, well, Cremona is a part of Italy where the finest, most prestigious violins in the world were made. Ah, was all she said. Oh, their locations are all well pinpointed, I said, but the Stainers, not so much.

She smiled, but she seemed absent. She must not have been very interested in what I was telling her. I could feel my head start-ing to spin, and I finished by saying, well, most of the Stainers ended up first in Austrian monasteries and then were sold to pri-vate collectors. I coughed a little, the cava's bubbles were tickling my throat. She urged me on, but Miss Anna told me that the violin was really hers. I nodded, and then I explained what had happened. I told her that I hadn't bought it, that I never would have been able to, that when I was a girl I lived in a world of utmost poverty, and I explained how and why that world was shattered. You know, the violin was magic, I added after another sip of cava.

I looked at her to see if I could tell how she was taking everything I'd been explaining. But she showed no emotion, not in the slightest. She was there, before me, with her eyes like saucers, staring into mine, as if she had never seen me before. I didn't know whether or not she was understanding what I was saying. Maybe she didn't believe it. I swear that I found the violin at the dump, I ended up saying at the sight of her sitting stock-still; you don't believe me? Then, she emerged from that static pose: oh, yes, I do believe you. She got up and said, excuse me for a moment, I'm going to the bathroom, I'll be right back.

When she returned, I could tell, from her expression, that the cava she had drunk hadn't sat well with her. And she'd had very little. I, on the other hand, had drank so much, and it was doing me a world of good. And now that the faucet of confessions had been opened, I didn't want to stop: Listen, but that's not all, I told her, half-forcing her to sit down and listen to me. She didn't put up a fight, her eyes were still wide, as if she'd just been dazzled by a camera flash. I told her about Anna and her father, I explained everything, everything. I let it all out, and in the end, the unburdening turned into grief and I ended up crying. I had never told anyone all that, and then I realized that I had kept it stored like a prickly ball inside me and that it would have been better to talk about it because that would have made it easier to overcome. Maria gave me some tissues and stroked my shoulder. I thought that she was a very good woman. She may not have understood the value of the instrument I'd found at the dump, but she did understand my tears and feelings. She wasn't like Anna, not at all.

Maria touching my shoulder like that, her gentle caress, reminded me of how Karl had asked me to hug him two days before he died. We all need human contact, we all need caresses to a greater or lesser extent, even when we act as if we don't. I didn't know then that Karl was at risk of dying, and I didn't know that the doctor had told him not to fly. I didn't know anything. And he, who did know it and who could tell he was at the end of his life, got up the next day and conducted a concert, and then boarded an airplane to Vienna. But first he asked me to hold him. Karl T. was human, too.

Mark

"Mark, listen, I didn't know anything about this!"

"Anna, leave me alone, just leave me be!"

We're making a scene in front of everyone. And with good reason. My wife is following me down the stairs to my dressing room, or more accurately, hounding me. And shouting that she knew nothing about this other violin. When the concert was over, Teresa, Anna, and I looked at the instrument. It is identical to the Stainer, down to the last detail, an exact copy, with the same color, the same little repaired flaw, everything. The only difference is that the signature isn't a Stainer. Inside the violin is the name of a luthier in Barcelona. I believe Anna, but I've had enough, this is the last straw. I don't know what happened, I don't know who could do such a thing to my wife, even though deep down I think she deserves it, but the rest of us didn't deserve it, after all, there are at least three of us who've been on the receiving end of this punishment, or, at least, the initial shock. The orchestra concertmaster also came over to have a look and ask us what had happened. We told him that we didn't know, and he had left after saying, the old switcheroo. He said it offhandedly, and I sensed a chuckle in his tone. He and the rest of the orchestra must be having a good laugh now, because the truth is they can't stand Anna.

"Mark, it's not my fault!"

"I know it's not your fault, but please, leave me alone!"

Our words, our shouts, echo off these whitish walls, and that huge abstract drawing halfway up the theater stairs suddenly strikes right at my soul. I don't know what the figures represent, all I can see in it are poorly rendered birds. What is going on, my God, what's wrong, why is everything so strange, why is everything so surreal? And Anna is obsessed with the waters of the Spree, she made me walk on the banks last night, and it was freezing, but she was riveted, looking down at the water, not listening to a word I said, she just watched the water and clung tightly to me. She clings to me because I'm the only one who can stand her, I'm her husband, I love her. Or I loved her.

I reach the door of my dressing room, turn around and blurt out, "Anna . . . why do you treat everyone like they're beneath you?"

I know that's not the question, that it has nothing to do with the violin, but this whole incident was the trigger that made me realize what's really going on. She is silent for a moment, surprised, and looks at me with transfixed eyes I now find cruel. Finally, she bites her lip and then, instead of answering, says, "I have something to tell you, Mark."

She says it in her usual seductress tone. The tone that made me fall into her clutches long ago, the tone she's used all this time to keep me tightly bound to her, I now realize. I inhale deeply and answer, "Fine, Anna, I have to tell you something, too—listen up: I've had it. This is over. I'm sorry, I can't take any more. I don't love you. I'm sorry."

That's it, I said it. I step into the dressing room. I can hear that she is still by the door with the fake Stainer in her hand, her gaze fixed on the nape of my neck, I can feel it stuck there, hers is a gaze that speaks of a life of suffering she was never able to overcome, which is now taking its toll. I turn and see that she wants to tell me something. She moves her lips, but in the end says nothing. She lowers her head, turns, and starts to walk away slowly. She holds on to the railing to go down the stairs. Goodbye, Anna.

Anna

It's not raining now, but the ground is slippery. I'm going to fall, I'm going to fall, I'm wearing stilettos. *En souffrant,* always *en souffrant.* And I forgot my coat, I left still dressed for the concert. I don't even know where I'm going, I don't know what I'm doing, I don't know what comes next now, I don't know what to do. I look at the ground, and even though it's dark, I try to make out the traces of water, those damp paving stones that are a threat to my balance in these heels. I kneel down and touch the cold, damp, gleaming ground with my fingertips. No, no, my soul isn't here, it's not possible, it's not here.

I didn't tell Mark. I didn't tell him that I'm expecting his child because then I would lose the child too. At the last moment, I held my tongue and that way the child will be all mine. Fine, then, I've lost Mark and the Stainer, but at least I'll have the baby, if all goes well, because I'm up in years, and I'll have to be careful, no excesses or risks.

And where is the Stainer, who's taken it? I look around me,

the audience has left, and there, in a corner, some members of the orchestra are laughing. Maybe they're the ones who switched the instruments. But it was an exact copy made in Barcelona, with premeditation. It was the Stainer but not, because you were fooled until you started to play it. When I picked it up from the chair where I'd put it down, I didn't notice any difference. And yet it was there where the change took place, where someone switched the silk purse for the sow's ear when I went out to get some fresh air and see the rain. This was done by someone who knows my habits. Yes, but who? It couldn't have been Teresa or Mark. Even though Mark has left me and as much as I hate Teresa, I don't think it was either of them. But if it wasn't them, then who was it? I can't think of anyone else, unless someone I don't know has followed me in order to steal my violin, and studied my moments, attending concert after concert for some time. Some dealer in antiques, and by now they must have sold the Stainer to someone for a king's ransom.

"Don't you think you should bundle up more, Anna?"

The voice came out of nowhere and gave me a start. I certainly wasn't expecting to turn and see Mama. She's even older, she's shrunken, she's just a slip of a thing with a scarf, hat, and coat. Suddenly, I have a suspicion and I just blurt it out, before even greeting her.

"Did you take my Stainer?"

She starts to laugh. "No, no. What could I do with a violin, or even the money I might get for it?"

Then she stops laughing and hesitates briefly before saying, "But I did hear that you weren't playing with your violin. I noticed a difference and I thought that something was wrong—they've stolen your Stainer, I see now."

I am silent. Of course, Mama noticed it too because, according to what she told me that day, even though we haven't talked since then, she's been coming to all my concerts. What devotion. Then she slowly added, "I came to talk to you because I see that you're having problems—"

"Don't tell me! Now you've come to help me solve them—do you know what's been my main problem since I was fourteen years old?"

I lashed out at her like that, I couldn't help myself. And now I see that she's crying. She covers herself with her scarf, but tears flow from her eyes, tears that gleam under the Berlin streetlights. I look at her carefully, and suddenly, I realize that she is no longer Mama, just an old lady crying because her conscience is so burdened that she can hardly bear it.

"Goodbye, I'm going to get my things." I say, just to say something. In fact, I don't know what to say, I don't know what to do.

And I turn around and start to walk. And then from behind me I hear: "Do you want me to wait for you?"

I stop. Something changes inside me, I don't know exactly what, but it is something that, all of sudden, disrupts the course of my life. I touch my belly, where there is a being I'll have to learn to understand. And I will have to do what Mama never did for me. But maybe I won't be so alone if—

"Anna—"

She has come to stand before me. I won't hug her, I can't. But I just discovered that there is a moment in life when all we have left is what's planted in front of us, and then we have to choose. Looking for the Indies and finding America. Mama is no longer Mama, she is an old woman who's emerged from the dark past, a woman who has dried her eyes and only has one treacherous tear slipping down her face. And when it lands on her scarf, it ceases to exist. And that happens just as I realize that in that tear is my soul, the soul I've been searching for over so many years.

As if we were coworkers who saw each other every day, I say, in a perfectly neutral tone, before entering the theater, "Please, wait for me—I'll be right out."

The
Peasant Girl
and the Shepherd

Maria

"Good morning, Maria, dear . . . Can you hear me? Good morning—"

Good morning, Mr. Karl. And *gut'n Tag, Herr* Beethoven. You're both here together, oh, how wonderful, Mr. Karl, don't look at me like that, you're making me blush. What lovely colored clouds, eh, they appear and disappear, they're like cotton balls. Like those colorful cotton balls used by one of the ladies I worked for before I came to live with you. And I had never seen them before, those were other times, and I thought I was having visions when, as I cleaned her bathroom, I found those soft little balls that were so different from the ones I was used to. They were so pretty . . . You, of course, never had any of those things. When I bought cotton balls for you, I bought the regular white ones, because I thought that if I bought them in colors you would ask me why I had, or you wouldn't recognize them as cotton balls. Because, you have to admit, Mr. Karl, for you it was always all about the music, little else. Well, okay, a few other things, that's true, and the big surprise came when I read your letter, Mr. Karl, my heart skipped a beat and, you know what, I didn't know how to react until they told me that you were dead. Then, of course, I didn't need to think it over any more, I didn't need the fifteen days you gave me to make a decision that I had already made anyway, because there are some decisions, Mr. Karl, that you don't make, decisions that you carry already etched on your heart, and no matter how hard you try to make another, there's no way around it.

And then, so many tears. I couldn't play the violin for a long time, you know, probably a year had already passed. At first I did try, when I still had the Stainer, when I still lived in your house, but I cried so, so much that I soon gave up. Later, in my new home, I tried again, I dusted it off and tried to play that song, but that didn't last long, soon I gave up trying to overcome the impossible to overcome. And I put the instrument down, next to Beethoven, they kept each other company and both got covered in dust. Every day I would stick my head into what had become a storage room, thinking today will be the day I can do it, and I tried to screw up my courage, and nothing came of it, and I would just shut the door again. And, when I went back there a year later, Beethoven, who was gray, had turned brown, and the violin case, which was dark brown, was then whitish.

"Maria, how are you? Don't move, just relax, I've taken care of everything, don't worry. Don't worry about a thing, dear . . . don't worry."

If the nurse says so, then everything is prepared and I won't worry anymore. I never would have thought I could do what I did. But there was no other way. Don't come back, Mr. Mark told me, because my wife would rather that . . . Mr. Mark couldn't get the words out because he was just making up an excuse to justify the fact that Mrs. Anna didn't want me around. Don't worry, I won't come back, I said, cutting off his stupid sentence that had gotten stuck on the way out of his mouth. He bit his lip and then he said, I'm sorry. Keep the keys, he said, as if he were doing me some big favor, adding, you never know. It was sad, he didn't know how to fix the situation, he didn't know what to do to avoid dumping me like that, like an old rag, without the possibility of returning to that house, to the apartment, as he called it. Now that was an apartment; it made mine look like a rabbit hole, because there was no comparison, his looked like a palace. Even though Mr. Mark had known hardship, it seems that living well was easy to get used to.

But what happened with Mark was later, I had already dusted off Beethoven in my little room in my little apartment, and gone back to playing the peasant girl and the shepherd, years before. I get the dates mixed up, I no longer know what happened when, and Mr. Karl, I get all the women that you entertained on the sofa mixed up, too. Those were other times, and when there were women on active duty, you didn't pay me any mind, and you forgot to teach me classes. Later, everything changed, but that was how it was at first, you remember, right? Don't try to change the subject, I'm not trying to admonish you for it, that's not it, but that's how it was, Mr. Karl, admit it. What's that? You didn't see me? I know you didn't see me, but don't worry, I always knew somehow, always. And I don't know if you saw me, but you seemed mad at me and you didn't say anything and you left, and, ay, I know, you already explained that in your letter. I know, Mr. Karl, when I read it, I started trembling all over. I was trembling all over, yes, I was. And I cried too, Mr. Karl, but not in sadness like when you died. Then there weren't these colorful clouds. There was no pointy tree. I had to go, I had to go. The tree was yellow, I saw it because the moon was bright and so I saw it, and that was where I put down the case and I started to play, and no one came, Mr. Karl, because it was very dark. And my stomach hurt so much, my stomach hurt so bad that in the end all of me was a ball of fire.

"Maria, how are you feeling?"

I would say fine, but I can't answer. I cannot speak, I only make a strange noise that comes out of where I felt the fire. Now that's it, I have no fire or anything inside, only peace, an unfamiliar peace that leads me to the paradise of the cottony clouds and the Beethovens that give me an unfriendly look, with one eyebrow raised. And beside them, you, yes, I know, Mr. Karl, no need to say more, I already know, I can see.

That one who speaks Catalan and Spanish came in, because all the other ones that come through speak that incomprehensible language and when they enter a room they say *gut'n Tag*. The first time I heard it, I made an enormous effort to open my eyes and see if there was a Beethoven in the room where they have me now. But no, there wasn't, just a TV and a chair and a wardrobe, all the color of an old smear. And I thought, *Where am I*, and I tried to remember, but at first I couldn't remember anything. Later, I did. And finally I was even able to speak to the one nurse who knows Catalan and Spanish, who told me that they had found me out cold on the ground in the middle of a square, with the violin by my side, and that I had been sleeping for three days, but that I didn't need to worry about anything, and that the violin was in the wardrobe. But I opened my eyes and I said I was worried.

Now everything is taken care of, Mr. Karl. After Miss Teresa told me where she'd found the violin, it was all easy as pie, because less than six months later, your son called me to ask for a favor. And, since I answered, as you wish, Mr. Mark, ay, sorry, Mark, he begged me to keep an eye on his apartment because he had to take Mrs. Anna to a spa for ten days, and he wasn't comfortable leaving the jewelry and the Stainer there alone for so many days, because the doctor had told him that they couldn't bring the violin with them, that Mrs. Anna had to forget she was a musician over those ten days. I think Mr. Mark didn't trust the maid that Mrs. Anna had hired, because he told me, come a couple of times, no one will be here, you'll be alone, and don't touch anything, eh, so they don't think that—he stopped short; when Mr. Mark talked to me, he would leave things half said, he didn't know how to finish them, and I felt sorry for him because he was too sincere, he was like you, he had to learn to be a bit more diplomatic. Don't worry, I said to reassure him. Thank you, Maria, he said immediately, you are worth more than all the jewelry and the Stainer put together. And I felt happy because I sensed him smiling at me on the other end of the line.

Honestly, it hadn't occurred to me before, but then a light went on in my head, a light like the one that lit up yesterday, or today, or ten days ago. I don't know, because I've lost all notion of time, a light like the one that made me ask the one nurse who knew Catalan and Spanish—when I could still speak—to please take a piece of paper and a pen and write this down, Miss Teresa, as you will see in the attached letter from Mr. Karl, the violin is mine, and I was the one who threw it out, and now I am giving it to you. And I signed as best I could and I said to the nurse, please, when I've passed on, send this note that we've just written, and this letter from the drawer on the bedside table and the Stainer, all together, to this address for Miss Teresa. The Stainer, repeated the nurse, with a confused expression. The violin that you put in the wardrobe. Oh, yes, she said, slightly disconcerted. That violin, it has a name, I said. I think, Mr. Karl, that that's the last thing of any length that I said, when I woke up at that point I don't know if it was now or before; oh, how time flies, and how strange it all is. And you have no idea how hard it was for me to say that many things in a row to the one nurse who could understand me. But I managed to do it and then I was at peace.

When I played the peasant girl and the shepherd again, by Beethoven's side, after a year of living in the small apartment, first I had to dust off the plaster musician and the violin's case. And then I had to tune the instrument. And there was a broken string, the E, and I rushed to find another. I knew a lot about that, remember, Mr. Karl, how you would send me to buy new strings, and how you taught me to replace them. And they were almost always E strings, because that's the one that always breaks. Well, you should know that I had no trouble replacing it, not that day and not on any other. Since then I've played that song, that one and the others, without crying, but with so much feeling that I left the world, with that soul that you always said I had, and I would close my eyes and I would see you, and when I opened them again, I thought that I would see you before me, but no, it was just pokerfaced Beethoven. And I didn't know if I had played it the way I should, because Beethoven was fine with everything.

Everything in that apartment was small. And in Mr. Mark's apartment, everything was big. Since I had spent a few years cleaning it, I knew it well, and I had little trouble finding the Stainer when I went there those days. I went straight for it, I had my plan all mapped out, I had gotten an idea in my head and I'm still not sure now whether it was a good one or a bad one, but, either way, what's done is done and I did what I had to do. I became methodical and precise, Mr. Karl. I quickly went to the place where I bought the strings and I asked them if they knew someone who made violins. And they said yes, and they gave me a card, and I went there, and I found a man who looked me up and down when I told him I needed a special violin and that he only had a week to make it. That man responded in a slightly sarcastic tone, asking whether I thought a violin was a toy or what. I said no, not at all, and that I would pay him a lot of money to make an exact copy of another violin in a week. And then I mentioned a figure, which was more or less a quarter of all the money you left me in your will. Well, it seems I made him an exorbitant offer because his eyes grew wide as plates and, after a second of shock, he slowly got out the words, this much in advance and this much when you pick it up. I said okay and the next day I brought him the Stainer, and I picked it up a week later.

The violinmaker, who at first had looked at me with distrust and mockery, was waiting for me with tea and cookies prepared, and he asked me to sit down and said things like, ma'am, I'll bring out your instrument in a moment, it's all ready, and I don't know what else. But I felt like getting back at him and I said, no, thanks, give me the Stainer and the copy, I want to have a good look at it, and if everything is as it should be, I'll pay you what I owe you and

I'll be on my way. And he bowed down to the floor, well, not to the floor, but almost, and then he went to find the violins and he brought them to me, and first I made sure that he hadn't done anything to the Stainer and I checked the signature and everything, looking through the long hole, and then I looked at the other instrument and, God, it was really identical to the Stainer, it was hard to tell the difference except for the signature, and the sound, of course. And I know because I played it a little bit in front of that violinmaker, who stood there with his mouth open. And, with his mouth still open, I paid him what I owed him, and said thank you and goodbye. And I returned the Stainer to Mark's house a day before they came back from their stay at the spa with his wife much better, and he called me to say, so, was everything in order? Everything in order, sir . . . I mean, Mark. I can never thank you enough for all you've done for me, Maria, he then said. No need, I replied, condescendingly, and to myself I thought, *you've already thanked me, you have no idea.*

The other violin also had soul, I discovered. Mr. Karl, I still don't understand how we can see violins' souls and not people's. But the form our souls take makes flying much easier, of course, and when mine leaves me it will rush off to find you. And, when we've found each other, we'll have hot chocolate with whipped cream in the kitchen of our house made of colorful clouds. And, if you'd like, you can have ladies on active duty, sir, it doesn't bother me at all. People can get used to anything. And it's been so many years.

I didn't know when I could switch one violin for the other, and a lot of time passed, and finally I thought that maybe I never would pull it off because I was getting old, but, well, at least I could pretend I was playing the Stainer because it really did look so much like it, and now I practiced with the new violin—and even though it wasn't the Stainer, it sounded good, very good. And when I'd pretty much accepted that I would never be able to get my violin back, because it is mine, because you gave it to me, well, when I thought I'd never get it back, Mr. Mark called me to tell me about the concert in Berlin and asked me to go, saying that it would please him very much. And I said, but what about Mrs. Anna? And it seemed he wasn't so hung up on her anymore, pfff, forget about her, he said, I want you to come. And I said no, and he said yes, and no and yes, and in the end the idea came to me and I said, okay, I'll come.

I was very tired and my stomach was starting to hurt. But just a little bit, and I didn't give it much importance. And, besides, I wanted to do the job, and I wanted to do it well. I remember that when I was planning it, I would sing that bit about, "Here I go, cleaning the house, cleaning up the whole house . . ." because Mr. Mark had told me that in Berlin they would play the Sunday morning music, that that was the whole point, and it had lyrics because I had added them, except then they didn't have the music in the background to go along with them. And one day, Mr. Karl, you know what, well, I went to a record store, and I asked if they had that music, and I sang a little bit of it, and the salesperson blushed and went to ask someone else who worked there, and finally the one in charge of classical music came over and said, oh, you mean the concerto for two violins, by Bach. Exactly, I exclaimed, because the part about the two violins fit perfectly with my idea, of course; you played that music with two violinists, so that must be it. And then I bought the record, actually it was one of those little ones, CDs they call them, one that I could play on my stereo, and I went home and from then on I had music to accompany my singing. But, Mr. Karl, every time I put on that Bach CD I would cry my eyes out because I could see you, standing there, big and tall, laughing and scooping up spoonfuls of hot chocolate, I don't know why I saw you laughing and scooping up spoonfuls of hot chocolate. Like now, I see you dipping your spoon in it again, it's as if you never do anything else, eh, you've never stopped doing it all these years, but I didn't make it for you this time, because I can't move, and I think I have something on my face, in my mouth and neck, right now I couldn't swallow a thing. Blessed Virgin of the Macarena, I wish they'd take these things off me for a little while and I would go with you, I'm fed up with all this. If I could move, I'd take them off myself and end this story, but I can't move, I can't manage to make the effort I need to rip out this tube for once and for all.

I bought a ticket for a flight one day earlier, and I told Mr. Mark that oh, I have a sister who lives in Berlin, and she told me to come the day before to spend some time with her. Of course, I have no sister here, I don't even have a sister, and all of my family stayed in Andalusia when I went up to Barcelona, but Mr. Mark believed it hook, line, and sinker. He asked me if I had a ticket, and I said I did. He told me that he had also bought one for me, but that I shouldn't worry, he could cancel it. But, Maria, you're full of surprises, he said, slightly chiding me, I didn't think you even knew how to buy a plane ticket. He told me over the telephone and I laughed a little as I thought, *Who do you think bought your father's tickets?* but I didn't say anything, no. I had gone to the agency, the same one as ever. I'd had to drag myself over there, that was a month ago, well, a month before I ended up here, of course. Because I don't know how long I've been here, I don't know if it's been an hour or twenty days or three months, oh, lord, I'm so exhausted and confused. And I found another travel agency closer to my house, but I wanted the one I'd always used, and I went there. And when I was there I looked to see if I knew anyone, and yes, there was still an older man who I knew, oh, he wasn't as old as you or I, Mr. Karl, but he was the man who'd replaced the woman who used to help me when she retired. And he helped me with everything, he gave me the tickets, both ways, apart from the group, because I don't even know how many people came to Berlin. Boy, it was like when you came with the whole orchestra, but I didn't buy the tickets then; it was too complicated. And the man at the travel agency, who had me sit down and treated me very well, he also found a hotel for me to stay in that one night before the others arrived.

And that was how we did it, Mr. Karl. Are you surprised? I can see that you're not. The day I came to Berlin I took the copy of the Stainer to the theater. I went there in a taxi, and they held it in the coat check for a modest price after a bit of back and forth in gestures with the girl in charge. In fact, I didn't know when to do the switch, but I had gotten it in my head that I would do it here, in Berlin, for you and for everything, and also because Miss Teresa has suffered so much in this life, poor thing. It's true that Miss Anna has also suffered, and maybe she's suffered more than any of us, but you'll agree with me that she needs to take a good fall so she can learn to get up again with a different attitude. Don't look at me like that, it cuts me to the quick, and deep down you know I'm right.

And they arrived the next day, and we all met up at the hotel, and Mrs. Anna made such a scene, you can't even imagine, it was as if I gave her a rash, and all I was doing was sitting in a chair because all the coming and going had left me worn out, and they were discussing the details of how and when they would rehearse and how they would get to the theater and all that. And that was when, at lunchtime on the first day, they mentioned in passing that Miss Anna had the habit of rehearsing in her dressing room before a performance and then, at the last minute, she would leave her violin by the stage entrance and go out for some air. She even blushed when someone laughed a little, because the orchestra, I saw that clearly, made fun of her all the time, laughing under their breath, and I don't know if she realized it. But she would lift her nose more and more, pointing it upward, and since hers is so narrow and small, it looked like a needle. I just don't know, Mr. Karl, how you could have her on active duty, because that woman is just so stuck-up. Anyway, I'm not going to reproach you for that now, don't worry.

The rest was more or less easy. I wasn't counting on not feeling well, that wasn't in my plans, and I started to feel very bad, Mr. Karl, really very bad, because my stomach was on fire and it was terrible, worse and worse, and sometimes I couldn't even breathe at all, but I had to last long enough to make the switch, and make it here, in Berlin, and I did it. When I had done it, I left because I could barely stand and I didn't want to hear Mrs. Anna's reaction when she started to play the Bach concerto. I had already had my fun, and that would have been too much, they would have found me dead right there in my seat, and that wouldn't be right. It seems rude to die in a theater, and I was dressed in a very, very fancy long dress that I think is here in the wardrobe too, next to the violin. So I left, I went by the coat check, got back the Stainer that I had left there earlier, planning to pick it up the next day, but in the end I took it with me. I picked it up because I couldn't take any more, Mr. Karl. Once I'd done what I had to do, I felt myself dying. I touched the letter, your letter, which I've been carrying with me ever since you gave it to me, the one that's now in the drawer of the bedside table, ready to be sent to Miss Teresa, and I won't tell you where I carried it because now I'm embarrassed. But you can imagine, and I said to myself that there was one more thing I needed to do before I left this world. And I stopped a taxi and I said, best I could, take me to Kollwitzplatz. And, I know it's hard to believe, but he understood me.

There was a tree with a pointy top, Mr. Karl, with a bench beneath it. A pretty tree, even though it was dark and had no real charm. I reached it along a path of leaves that blew up into the air with each step because I couldn't lift my feet off the ground. The violin weighed heavily on me, I didn't know how this would end, but I knew what I had to do.

There, beneath the pointy yellow tree, I began to play the peasant girl and the shepherd. I could barely breathe, I could barely move, my whole body was in pain, but I put the violin on my shoulder, the violin that Mrs. Anna had tuned perfectly. Everything was wet, but it wasn't raining and the moon had risen, round as an orange, a moon that caressed my face as if it were your hand, as if you were stroking me yourself. I closed my eyes and I played the Stainer. The violin did its magic, and all of a sudden, I was no longer in that park but beside the piano, in the living room, with you. And I imagined myself dressed up as a peasant girl, and you dressed as a shepherd. The hot tears warmed my freezing cheeks, because you know, Mr. Karl, this city of yours is the city of cold. And I couldn't stop crying. And the song continued, to its end. And, when it was finished, you got up and came by my side and you said, take off your uniform, please.

And I don't know anything more than that, I don't know what happened. Now, look, I've managed to open my eyes. There is no one here and now that I've regained some consciousness, I realize that, with a bit of effort, I can pull out this tube that's so uncomfortable. I'm going to give it a try. If I succeed, Mr. Karl, I'll come to be with you forever among the colorful clouds, and not even my soul will be left down here.

Maria,

I'm not one for writing letters. I only write music and I'm not sure I can even remember how to string together an entire line. But there is something that I want to tell you and I haven't dared in all this time, so I finally opted to write it out on this paper and, since I'm such a coward, I'll give it to you right as I'm leaving for a few days.

The violin that you threw onto the garbage cart by mistake forty years ago is now yours. I got it back for you. Keep it and play those German songs you play so well, as often as you can, especially the one about the peasant girl and the shepherd. You play with a delicacy that I've never heard from anyone else, ever. And all you were missing was a violin like the Stainer. When my father brought it back from Salzburg and gave it to me, I never imagined it would end up in the hands of someone who made it sound so lovely. Yes, I know that you don't have the agility or the perfect technique of other violinists because you haven't had the opportunities that other musicians have had. But you do have what many would kill for: the ability to leave breathless whoever listens to you play. Like me, for example. You've made me cry, Maria, and you don't know how hard it is to make a musician cry . . .

But that's not what I wanted to tell you. What I wanted to tell you, Maria, is that you have captured my soul. Perhaps that's why you play so well: because you have two souls, mine and your own. For forty years you have moved silently by my side, you've made me feel so at home in this house, you've made sure I never lacked for anything, you've made me that exquisite hot chocolate that I enjoy mostly for the pleasure of some time conversing with you . . . you who've laughed and cried with me . . . you have truly touched my heart. I realized it the first day when you played our song so beautifully . . . the day I asked you to take off your uniform. I had to leave to keep from taking it off myself, it was very hard for me to hold myself back. Imagine what you would have thought of me if I had, if I'd taken off your uniform right there, when you already think God knows what about the way I live my life . . . Maria, I've tried to get you out of my head, but I cannot. And this is the first time that's ever happened to me: I met my wife when I was very young and in special circumstances. I fell in love, that's true, but I don't know if I was drawn into it by the atmosphere and by everything that was happening around us in those days. And all the other women who I've slept with have been nothing more than moments of musical intensity . . . it was like changing tone in the same composition . . . I don't know if I'm explaining myself well, and I don't know if you've ever fully understood it, but I don't know how to say it any other way. But, with you, recently, I've had to stifle my desire to kiss your hands and your face and your everything, every day, and my desire to tell you how I feel. My desire to tell you that I love you. Forgive my honesty, it's how I feel and I can no longer keep it to myself, even though I don't dare say it to your face.

I am leaving and I hope to return. Right now I feel very well. They've told me that traveling could suddenly ruin my fragile health, but you know how doctors are, they're always exaggerating . . . and I feel up to it. So you have fifteen days to think it over . . . And, when I return . . . will you please give me an answer? We are both old enough and we know each other so well! I no longer want to be with any other women, if that is what worries you—even though I don't think that's ever been much of an issue for you. If you say yes, I'd like to take you to my Kollwitzplatz . . . We'll travel to Berlin and we'll bring the Stainer with us and you can play the song about the peasant girl and the shepherd there where I used to play . . . And I will feel proud of having taught you a few notes that you could put soul into, the soul you've carried inside you ever since your parents taught you to sing what I wouldn't let you. And I will hold you close and we will be happy, Maria.

But . . . don't worry, because, if you don't want to be with me . . . I mean, more than you have been up until now . . . if you don't want anything more, I promise that I will keep the distance that you deserve and respect your decision, keeping the distance that we have maintained between us over the course of these forty wonderful years.

Yours always,
KARL

P.S. Oh, I forgot to mention: I promised Anna that I'd marry her, in exchange for the violin. Don't worry about that, I'll marry her, but we'll be rid of her soon enough: As soon as she sees how little attention I pay her, she'll leave me.

about the author

Blanca Busquets is a Catalan writer and radio journalist. She began writing at the age of twelve and has published seven novels, which have been translated into Spanish, Italian, German, Russian, Polish, Norwegian, and French. Her fifth novel, *La Nevada Del Cucut*, was the winner of the 2011 Catalan Booksellers' Prize. She lives in Barcelona, Spain.

Mara Faye Lethem has translated novels by Jaume Cabré, David Trueba, Albert Sánchez Piñol, Javier Calvo, Patricio Pron, Marc Pastor, and Toni Sala, among others. These books have been featured as *New York Times* and *Booklist* Editors' Picks, and among the Best Books of the Year in *The Times* and Readers' Favourite Books in the *Financial Times*. Her translation of *The Whispering City*, by Sara Moliner, recently received an English PEN Award.